AMAZON.COM

NOW & THEN

JOHN LOCKE

HEAD
of ZEUS

This edition first published in the UK in 2013 by Head of Zeus Ltd

Copyright © John Locke, 2010

9 7 5 3 1 2 4 6 8

A CIP catalogue record for this book is available from
the British Library.

ISBN (Paperback): 9781781852361
ISBN (eBook): 9781781852378

Printed and bound by CPI Group (UK) Ltd, Croydon, CR0 4YY

Head of Zeus Ltd
Clerkenwell House
45-47 Clerkenwell Green
London EC1R 0HT

www.headofzeus.com

For my mother, Maurine, the remarkable woman who has been a life-long inspiration to me: I have finally written a book that contains less than two-dozen truly dirty words.

FOREWORD

There are people in this world who move through our lives quietly, unassumingly, who, seeking nothing in return, take away our pain.

PROLOGUE

Twelve Months Earlier…

THE YOUNG REPORTER'S name was Joe, and he was unhappy about the assignment. He had to interview the lead in a college play and try to make the segment interesting enough to fill two minutes on the local TV news. He'd rather be covering a murder or congressional scandal, but Joe was new to the station, and dues had to be paid. He'd come here tired and his back was killing him from the elbow shot he'd taken in last night's rugby game.

When Libby Vail entered the room he showed her where to sit, and after the camera guy spent a few minutes checking the lighting, Joe tried to sound like he gave a shit about the interview.

But he didn't.

It was such a small-town production, and Libby, while certainly adequate for this role, was an unlikely candidate for Broadway stardom. As Joe slogged through the list of bullshit questions, he couldn't help but notice the light tingling in his back where the pain had been. As the pain dissipated, a feeling of euphoria began sweeping over him. Were the anti-inflammatories finally kicking in?

Just before wrapping up, he said, "Tell me something about you that few people know."

Libby Vail's face grew animated. She looked from side to side, as if sharing a scandalous secret.

"Well," she said, "Don't tell anyone, but I'm a direct descendant of Jack Hawley, the pirate."

Joe gave her a confused look.

"Gentleman Jack Hawley?" Libby said.

"Sorry, never heard of him."

Libby giggled. "Oh well."

Joe signaled the cameraman to pack his gear.

"Sorry I wasn't more interesting," Libby said.

Joe took a moment to glance at her. Was she pouting over her complete snooze of an interview? She didn't appear to be. He studied her a moment longer and decided Libby Vail was a pretty little thing, frail, with big green eyes and an expressive face.

"You did fine," he said.

"Really?"

Joe prepared to ease himself to a standing position but suddenly realized there was no "easing" necessary. His back was completely fine. There had to be something more at work here than anti-inflammatories. Crazy as it seemed, there was something about being near Libby Vail that made him feel stronger, more energetic. Without giving a second thought to his former back injury, he took up a swashbuckling pose, pretended to cut a swath of air with his imaginary sword. Then he removed his pen and note pad from his pocket and started to write.

"Jack Hawley, you said?"

Libby's laugh spilled out of her smile. "*Gentleman* Jack Hawley."

She stood and brandished her own imaginary sword, struck a pirate's pose, and said, "Arrr!"

Joe laughed and said, "Aye, Aye, wench. That just might be the angle this story needs."

That night his station ran the story.

Three days later he had an even better story:

Libby Vail had gone missing.

PART ONE

NOW

1.

IT WAS ONE of those arguments you could see coming a mile away.

"Things are going great between us," Rachel said.

I nodded, warily.

We were on the porch swing of The Seaside, a bed and breakfast in St. Alban's Beach, Florida. It was early evening, and the light summer breeze from the ocean kept the mosquitoes at bay. We'd had dinner at Chez Vous, a pretentious little grease pit on Cane Street, and though I'd rate our meal somewhere between appalling and insulting, neither of us seemed worse for the fare.

"You love me," Rachel said.

"I do."

"And I'm fun, right?"

"Undeniably."

"Just imagine how much fun we'd have if we lived together!"

I didn't respond, didn't so much as lift an eyelid.

"Kevin?"

"Mmm?"

"What do you think?"

It was one of those moments when you have to be honest or happy, and you can't be both.

"Kevin?"

A train rumbled faintly in the distance. Rachel's head was in my lap. She looked up at me, studying my face, as I rocked the swing with my feet.

"Kevin?"

Rachel knows my name is Donovan Creed, but she'd met me as Kevin Vaughn, and she's comfortable calling me that, so I don't make a big deal out of it.

"Know what I think?" I said.

"What's that, honey?" she purred.

"I think things are perfect just the way they are."

Her body stiffened a half-second before reacting—a useful bit of information to file in my brain, since my continued existence often comes down to knowing such details. Compared to most humans, a half-second is quick. In my line of work (I kill people) it's a lifetime.

Literally.

So Rachel was painfully slow by my standards, a good thing, since her bipolar personality dysfunction had become more pronounced each day of our vacation, occasionally leading to sudden violent outbursts. I love dating her, but my life could be in danger with a live-in relationship. As long as I remain conscious, she can't seriously harm me. But if we were to live together I'd eventually have to sleep, and all bets would be off.

"You're a fucking bastard and I don't want to see you, ever again!" Rachel shrieked.

She jumped off my lap and launched her hand toward my face. I could have easily avoided the slap, but it had been weeks since I'd sparred, and I missed the physical contact. She smacked me two, three times, grabbed her purse, slung it over her shoulder, and stomped off into the dusk.

Rachel had been slightly unstable even before she'd been

locked in a Lucite container for two days and nights. I busted her out, what, two weeks ago? Since then we'd been on vacation, making our way down the Atlantic coast, hitting all the beaches of consequence, while her mental condition steadily deteriorated.

You may be wondering how I managed to catch a few hours of sleep while traveling with Rachel.

Simple: I drugged her.

So sure, I could move in and live with Rachel, bring my pills and knock her unconscious every night, but in the long run that's no basis for maintaining a healthy relationship.

I closed my eyes and listened to her cuss a blue streak as she moved down the road. Her fury was almost poetic, as sudden and dangerous as a cyclone. She was heading north on A1A toward Amelia Island Plantation, the place where my associate, Callie Carpenter, and I killed a woman named Monica Childers five years ago.

2.

ANGRY OR NOT, Rachel was kickass sexy in that mouth-watering, leave-your-wife sort of way, with long brown hair; blonde highlights, and eyes the color of tupelo honey.

I let her get a half-mile down the road before starting after her. When we'd gone about a mile, I moved to within three feet and remained behind her, matching her pace, giving her space in case she wasn't ready to talk. I shadowed her like that until I suddenly felt something that's hard to describe. It was a type of serene presence, like a drug-induced high, but calming and blissful. One minute I'm normal, the next I'm practically euphoric, and then it passed.

Rachel felt it too.

She stopped abruptly, but didn't turn around.

"Am I crazy, Kevin?"

"You might be the sanest person I know," I said, thinking that was a sad thing to have to admit.

"I'm sorry I hit you."

"That was a million years ago."

She turned and put her arms around me and kissed my mouth. Then we turned it into a full body hug, right there in the middle of the highway.

It was a quiet night, the cars few and far between, and we headed back toward the bed and breakfast. The tall grass on the shoulders swayed in the breeze, and I kept us in the middle of the road so the ticks wouldn't get on her legs.

The feeling of serenity—or whatever it was—lasted maybe ten seconds, and yet it had been powerful enough to make me want to pursue its source. Could there have been something in the air? Some type of flower whose aroma was intoxicating? Either we had moved through a space where it was, or it had invaded our space and moved on. I made a mental note to thoroughly check the area the next morning when I went on my run.

Rachel said, "You remember a couple of weeks ago when Karen said you were a killer, not a thief?"

"Her real name is Callie," I said.

Rachel didn't respond, so I added, "Yeah, I remember."

"What did she mean?"

Rachel knew I worked for Homeland Security, but so far I hadn't felt the need to tell her that my job involved assassinating suspected terrorists. Nor did I happen to mention that in my spare time I was a contract killer for the mob.

"She was probably talking about my killer smile," I said.

"I wonder."

I looked at her but didn't say anything.

She said, "The way you handled yourself when you saved me and Sam from those guys. Not to mention Lou."

"Lou Kelly? What about him?"

"You can tell Lou's a tough guy."

"He is."

"But he was afraid of you and Karen. And Karen hit Sam with one punch and nearly killed him."

"So?"

Rachel took my hand in hers, put it to her lips.

"I'm not wearing panties," she said.

I took a moment to marvel at her facility for random

discourse.

"Always useful information for a boyfriend to have," I said.

At that moment, for no apparent reason, she bit the shit out of my hand. I wondered briefly if she was really crazy or just messing with me.

"I never wear panties," I said.

"Did you feel it just now when I bit you? 'Cause you never yelled or anything."

"Was that you?" I said. "Yeah, I felt it."

"That's why I love you so much," Rachel said.

"Because I don't yell when you bite me?"

"No, 'cause you're funny."

"Good to know," I said, rubbing my hand.

"I bet you've got a hell of a history, Kevin."

"I won't deny it."

"Maybe someday you'll tell me," she said.

"Maybe I'll write a book."

She smiled. "If you do, will you put me in it?"

"Of course."

"You promise?"

"If I write a book, I'll put you in it. I'll call it *Now and Then*."

"I hope you're not married to that title," she said, "or you'll never make the first sale."

It was getting dark. Lights in the beach rentals up and down the highway began popping on. In front of us, to the left, a little boy with a buzz cut raced onto the balcony of a two-story, pulled his pants down to his ankles and tried to pee through the rail. His mother yelped and caught him in the nick of time and dragged him back through the sliding glass door. By then they were both laughing.

Rachel and I smiled at each other.

"Kids," I said.

"Boys, you mean."

I looked at her. "What, you're saying girls don't pee outdoors?"

"Not from heights."

We walked in silence while I pondered the validity of her remark.

Rachel said, "I haven't told my mom."

"Told her what?"

"About us."

"What about us?"

"About us getting married, silly."

"Oh, that," I said.

"Maybe I should tell her in person," she said.

"That's probably a good idea."

We'd come to an open area, maybe eighty yards from the nearest house. I heard a car coming up behind us, moving slowly. I instinctively moved Rachel to the left side of the road.

"You dudes need a ride?"

Several of them in the car: blue, 69 Camaro Super Sport, dual white racing stripes on the hood.

The driver had done the talking. He was Rachel's age, meaning late twenties. He had a chipped front tooth, and greasy, stringy hair. His eyes had the glazed look of a pot-head who took his weed seriously. When the back window zipped down, a cloud of smoke leaked out and swirled in the breeze.

An alarmingly ugly guy with thick lips said, "We'll give the girl a ride." Addressing Rachel, he said, "Hey chica, you want a little strange? Climb in. We'll give you a ride you won't never forget!"

"Back off, fuckwad," Rachel said. "Or my fiancé will kick your ass."

The ugly guy's eyelids were at half-mast. He showed me a dull, vacant stare. "That right, pops?"

"Move along," I said.

"You believe this shit?" he said to someone in the back seat. "Bitch turning down our sweet ride. Pops prob'ly got a Oldsmobile nearby. Maybe we drive around, see we can find it. Maybe we torch that motherfucker for you, eh pops?"

I returned his stare. "Like the lady said: I want a ride, I'll kick your ass and take your car."

The scumbags in the car erupted like Springer's audience when Jerry trots out the trailer trash. There were numerous threats hurled in our direction, and someone in the back seat on the far side—a kid with a colorful bandana—lifted himself out the window and aimed a gun at me sideways.

It was dusk, but not too dark for me to get a good look at the piece.

"Be careful with that thing," I said.

"Ha! You ain't so brave now, are you, pops?"

"Braver," I said. "That piece of shit gun is all wrong. No way it fires without blowing up in your face."

"You want, I'll shoot it now."

"I'd pay to see that," I said, "but I got a question."

"What's that, asshole?"

"You think your friends will take your body to the hospital, or just dump you here on the road?"

The kid looked at his gun.

"Fuck you!" he said, and climbed back in the car.

The driver said, "Another time, pops."

"What's wrong with right now?" I said.

"Another time."

He hoisted his arm out the window and gave us the finger. They laughed and roared away.

"You think they'll come back?" Rachel said.

"I hope so," I said.

3.

THE YOUNG MAN was lying on his back on a sand dune thick with saw grass. Few people knew him. Those who did called him D'Augie.

D'Augie had followed Creed and Rachel from a careful distance. When D'Augie saw them speaking, he knew they were about to turn and head back to the bed and breakfast, which is why he got a running start and dove into the sand dune, face first. After waiting a moment, he rolled onto his back and heard a car full of punks pull up to the couple, heard what sounded like smack talk, but he was too far away to discern the words. When the car drove noisily away, D'Augie kept still, slowed his breathing, and relaxed his body until it virtually melted into the sand dune. He touched the knife in his pocket with his right hand.

He'd be using it soon.

Lying on the sand dune, D'Augie was, for all intents and purposes, invisible. The breeze coming off the ocean blew sand crystals into his face, but D'Augie didn't twitch. He was one with nature, and nothing had the power to affect him.

D'Augie began a mental chant: *Lay here, wait till they pass, then jump up and kill Creed. Lay, wait, jump, kill. Lay, wait, jump—*

Some type of insect—an ant, probably—found an unguarded whisper of skin above one of his socks and began crawling up his leg.

Unfortunate, D'Augie thought, *but hardly a threat to my willpower.*

D'Augie knew Creed and Rachel were approaching the part of the road he'd occupied moments earlier. It wouldn't be long, a minute maybe.

D'Augie's pants were baggy, and he was wearing boxers—a combination of clothing that provided the insect a bare-skinned freeway all the way to his waist, should it care to journey that far. D'Augie wasn't dwelling on it, but he seemed to feel every step the insect made as it crawled past his knee and up his thigh.

Within seconds, a dozen more insects formed a line and began a steady march up his leg. D'Augie ignored them until there were more than thirty of the bastards crawling all over his testicles. He was finding it increasingly hard to remain one with nature. He wanted to scream, wanted to jump to his feet, throw off his clothes, and get the fuck off the sand dune.

But he couldn't. Creed and Rachel had been making steady progress, and were practically on top of him. He could hear their footsteps on the asphalt. To be precise, he heard only Rachel's feet, since Creed moved over the pavement as soundlessly as D'Augie himself had moved earlier.

D'Augie strained to hold his position. If he could remain perfectly still for another thirty seconds he could escape detection. Creed and Rachel would pass him, then D'Augie could spring up and catch Creed by surprise, slice his throat, and decide what to do with Rachel after ridding himself of these goddamned insects.

But Creed and Rachel didn't walk past him. They stopped just short of his position.

Shit!

Could they have noticed him?

D'Augie didn't think so. Though he was a scant fifteen feet from the road, it was practically dark and the saw grass where he lay was nearly three feet high. The sea oat clusters all around him were bending in the breeze, providing additional camouflage.

So no, they couldn't have seen him.

But something made them stop.

D'Augie felt another wave of insects crawl up his leg. *How many more?* he wondered. *Fifty? A hundred?*

Too many to count.

He heard Creed and Rachel kiss.

Then-O*h my God!*—suddenly his nuts were on fire!

Christ, it hurt.

It felt—

Christ, Almighty!

It felt like someone had built a fire in his lap and sent a bunch of bees to put it out.

The pain was horrific. D'Augie's body started to twitch and tremble. His face contorted involuntarily. His eyes became slits, and his upper lip peeled away, exposing his entire top row of teeth. D'Augie bit his lower lip so hard he drew blood. Then he opened and closed his mouth, faster and faster, raising and lowering his teeth, sinking them into his mangled lip again and again—until he realized this activity was only making things worse.

Lying there with his upper teeth exposed, clenched against his lower lip, D'Augie imagined he looked like a lounge lizard doing the "white man overbite" dance. Except that he wasn't dancing. He'd love to be dancing, hopping around, squishing the bugs—but he couldn't move. He couldn't move because he knew he couldn't beat Creed from the front. He wanted to move. *Had* to move! But he couldn't. D'Augie squeezed his eyelids together, and tears poured out, slid down the sides of his face, pooled in his ears.

The pain was intolerable.

Otherworldly.

D'Augie was being eaten alive.

What the fuck kind of bugs *were* these? It was as if they'd burrowed a centimeter into his flesh and laid a dozen acid eggs. Then the eggs exploded into flame at the same time. This was worse than bee stings, a million times worse, because it wasn't a "one and done" burn. No, these little fuckers tore into his skin like shark on chum. They bit and kept on biting or stinging or whatever the hell they were doing to him and he was trembling and shaking and chattering his teeth and—

And his nuts were swelling at an alarming rate, which seemed only to serve the purpose of creating a larger area to accommodate the reinforcement bugs. The more they bit, the more his nuts swelled, and this ever-expanding battlefield encouraged a hundred more insects to join the assault.

Get out of here! he silently screamed to Creed. *For the love of God, keep walking down the road!*

The woman said, "Kevin, let's do it right here."

What?

No! D'Augie thought. *Please God, don't let them do it right here! Twenty feet. Do it twenty feet down the road. Give me twenty feet and I'll kill them before they get their pants off.*

Creed said, "Best offer I've had all day. But there's gravel on the road, and possibly broken glass. You might get cut."

D'Augie didn't know why she was calling Creed Kevin, and he didn't care. All he could think about was how his nuts were twice their normal size and how the motherfuckers wouldn't stop stinging him. His testicles hurt so bad he almost didn't feel the insects stinging the rest of his privates.

Almost didn't.

Holy Shit!

D'Augie's insides began churning. He needed to vomit. Started to vomit, but swallowed back the bile. The contents of his stomach lurched, preparing for a second attempt. D'Augie realized he was having an allergic reaction to the venom from the bites or stings. Itchy welts were forming on his face and forehead. His upper chest throbbed. His throat started closing up. His eyelids fluttered. Barely conscious, slipping fast, he heard Rachel say:

"We could fuck on one of these sand dunes!"

…And heard Creed answer:

"Not in a million years."

…And Rachel:

"Why not?"

…And Creed:

"Fire ants."

…And then D'Augie passed out.

4.

"YOU HEAR THAT?" I said.

"What, the ocean?" Rachel said.

"More like something in the dune. You got a flashlight in your purse?"

"No. Wait, I've got a mini light on my car keys, will that work?"

I waited while she unsnapped the light, then took it from her.

"Stay here," I said.

I moved through the near-darkness, found the man lying on the sand dune. I kicked his ribs. No response. I leaned over him, flashed her mini light on his face.

"What's there?" Rachel said.

"A kid. Young man, early twenties."

"Is he dead?"

"Dead or dying. His body's crawling with fire ants."

"You think he's in shock?" she said, looking at him over my shoulder.

"Shock?"

"Anaphylactic shock. Like maybe he's having an allergic reaction?"

"Could be," I said. I grabbed his collar and dragged him to the side of the road.

Rachel fumbled in her purse a couple of seconds and pulled

21

something out.

"What's that?" I said.

"An EpiPen. It's for allergic reactions."

She handed me the pen and I gave her the mini light. She said, "There's a syringe inside. Take the cap off, hold the pen in your fist, and jab it in his thigh till you hear a click. Then hold it there for ten seconds."

"You've done this before?"

"A thousand times."

"Really?"

"No. But I read the directions."

I yanked his pants down to his knees.

"Ten seconds?" I said. "Any magic to that number?"

"That's how long it takes to enter the bloodstream and get absorbed by the muscles."

"You got your cell phone handy?"

She did, and used it to call 911. I injected as she calmly gave the dispatcher our location and explained the patient's condition.

"We gave him a dose of epinephrine," she said, "and we're about to start CPR."

That sounded like a good idea to me, so I slapped the fire ants off the kid's clothes as best I could, then his face. Then I tore his shirt open and killed a bunch more of them, and started CPR.

"Pull his shorts off," I said.

"Excuse me?" Rachel said.

"Strip him down. He's literally crawling with fire ants. We've got to get them off his body."

Rachel put the pen light in her teeth and tugged his boxers off.

"*Jesus Christ!*" she said.

"What?"

She aimed the beam at his crotch, and I looked at the kid's nuts. They were swollen to the size of avocados and covered with red, circular welts.

And scores of fire ants.

"Slap the ants off his dick," I said.

She raised her hand tentatively, poised to strike, then started to retch.

"How about we trade places," she gasped.

"His mouth's kind of mangled," I warned.

"Still," Rachel said.

We traded places. She gave him CPR, and I slapped the kid's crotch and thighs like they owed me money. When Rachel paused a moment, I pushed him on his side and slapped the ants on his back and ass for good measure. Then I eased him onto his back and she started in again with the CPR.

"That was so *creepy*," Rachel said, while pumping the kid's chest.

"Creepy?"

"His nuts."

"Uh huh."

"You ever see anything that creepy?" she said.

"The Grady Twins."

"The Grady twin boys?"

"Girls."

"Hmpf," Rachel said.

We worked on him till the ambulance arrived. While the two-man crew checked him out, I shook out his pants and shorts, and a large buck knife fell out and skittered across the pavement. I retrieved the knife and put it in my pocket. Then I put his clothes in a ball and tossed them on the front seat. While one of the EMS guys covered the kid in a blanket, the other took down some contact information from Rachel. They placed him in the ambulance, thanked us, and rushed him to the hospital.

Rachel and I stood still a minute before resuming our walk.

"You get stung?" I said.

"I don't think so."

"You'd know if you had."

"I guess. How about you?" she said.

"I'd feel better if we patted each other down."

She laughed. "You're just looking for an excuse to touch my boobs."

"How easily you see through me."

We brushed each other's clothing in the dark until satisfied we weren't transporting any ants to the B&B, then started walking.

"You were fantastic back there," I said.

"When?"

"The whole time."

"Tell me."

"You knew what to do, and you never hesitated. You were completely lucid and rational."

Dusk had become night, and though I couldn't see it, I'm sure she smiled.

"I have my moments," Rachel said.

We were quiet a while. I finally asked, "How'd you happen to have the syringe?"

"I carry it in my purse all the time."

I knew this to be untrue. Until just recently, Rachel and her husband, Sam, had lived in a huge house in Louisville, Kentucky. Unbeknownst to Rachel, I'd lived in their attic off and on for the past two years, during which time I'd routinely gone through her purse and their medicine cabinets, documenting every detail of their lives, checking their medications. I knew Rachel's medical history, or thought I did.

"How long have you been carrying this particular syringe?" I said.

"I got it in Savannah, at the drugstore."

"Don't you need a prescription?"

"Not when you've got a smile like mine!"

I knew about the smile. What I didn't know was if she'd been planning to kill me with the syringe.

"Why'd you get it?" I said. "Seriously."

"When I was a kid I got stung by fire ants," she said. "In the drug store in Savannah, a guy was saying how bad they were this year. I wanted to be ready in case one of us got stung on the beach."

That's the funny thing about Rachel. When she wasn't being crazy, she was quite capable.

We kept walking. I could tell she wanted to ask me something. Finally she did.

"Are you allergic to anything?"

"Cheesecake."

"What?"

"It makes me fat."

She might have muttered the word "asshole" under her breath.

We walked some more, and I said, "Nicotine."

"You don't smoke."

"Still, it's a poison. If you distill it and concentrate it to its purest essence, it's one of the deadliest poisons on earth."

"Is that the little black one in your kit?"

I keep a poison kit in my belongings. It's essential in my line of work. I'd made the mistake of warning Rachel about it early in the vacation when I'd caught her about to dab some Ricin on her wrist, thinking it was part of my cologne collection. When asked why I carried a kit filled with poisons, I came up with the bullshit excuse that I was delivering it to the Justice Department in Miami.

"You need to stay out of that kit."

"Fine, don't worry. But is it the black one?"

"It's the clear one, in the vial."

"That's the one that can kill you?"

"It is." Though it was the clear one in the vial, like most poisons, I had built up an immunity to it over time. The only poison I'm unable to handle is Tetrodotoxin, or TTX. Of course, I would never tell Rachel that, nor would I carry TTX in my kit. I love Rachel, but I couldn't trust her not to kill me.

"You must really trust me to tell me about your Kryptonite," she said.

"Of course. How can a relationship thrive without trust?"

After a few minutes we were able to make out the lights and wrought-iron balcony of The Seaside Bed and Breakfast. The balcony's ironwork was famous, unique, and more than a hundred and fifty years old. It had been handcrafted in Boston and shipped to St. Alban's Beach by rail. The architect who designed it was murdered in the alley behind the local bar the very night the installation had been completed. Local legend had it that the original owner of the Seaside had the architect killed so he wouldn't be able to replicate the design elsewhere.

I said, "After we shower I thought I'd take the rental car to the hospital to check on the kid."

"I'll come with you."

"Just to recap," I said. "We'll go inside, strip down, make

sure we've gotten rid of all the ants, take a hot shower, make wild, passionate love, then drive to the hospital."

"Whoa, cowboy," she said.

"Whoa?"

"On the sex part."

"Why?"

"You owe me an explanation. And an apology."

"For what?"

"You said a relationship can't flourish without trust."

"I said that?"

"You did."

"Then I stand by it."

"Prove it."

"Okay. How?"

"That comment you made about the Grady Twins."

"What about it?"

"I don't care how creepy they were. If you've had a threesome, I have a right to know the details."

I laughed.

"Laugh now, pay later," she said. "I'm not kidding, Kevin."

"Heeeere's Johnny!"

"Excuse me?"

"You know the movie, *The Shining*?" I said. "Jack Nicholson?"

"Uh huh."

"Remember the kid on the tricycle?"

She thought a minute.

"The one in the hotel that's riding up and down the hallways?"

"Right, the caretaker's son."

"Yeah, I remember. So what?"

"So he's riding down the hall a hundred miles an hour and

he suddenly sees the two girls and nearly shits his pants, remember?"

"Oh, God, yes!"

"The Grady Twins," I said.

5.

THE NORTHEAST FLORIDA Medical Center is located on Fifth Street, St. Alban's Beach. We were standing outside the kid's room, talking to the attending physician, Dr. Carstairs.

"How is he?" Rachel said.

"Too soon to tell, but he's on a ventilator, so he's got a chance. Thanks to you folks and the luck of St. Alban's."

"A doctor who believes in luck?" I said.

"We've lost very few patients since I've been here. I'd call that lucky, wouldn't you?"

"Some might be inclined to give you the credit."

"They'd be kind to do so. But there's something more at work here."

"Such as?"

"The patients here have the best attitudes I've ever seen. They eat more, sleep better, complain less, and most important, they believe they're going to improve."

"I don't know if I'd call it lucky," I said. "Miracle might be a better word."

"Then let's put it this way," he said. "If you're going to get sick or injured anywhere in the country, this appears the best place to be. And not because of me."

Dr. Carstairs was short and squat, late forties. His head was completely bald in the middle, and he'd grown his fringe hair long enough to form a short pony tail in back.

"Incongruous," Rachel whispered, trying out a word I'd taught her months ago, when she first started cheating on her husband.

"Compensatory displacement," I whispered back.

She arched an eyebrow and I wanted to take her right there. She caught my look and smiled, then turned back to face the doctor. While she looked at him I studied her profile, and—okay, I know it's corny—but time seemed to freeze. Rachel nodded her head, responding to something the doctor had said, and I realized I'd been focusing on her sexuality so intently, I'd missed it. Rachel somehow managed to keep her focus on the doctor despite my sexuality. What willpower she must have!

"Sensitization?" Rachel said.

"That means he had to have been stung by fire ants at least once in the past, probably as a child. The first stinging event often fails to cause an allergic reaction. But the second can be deadly."

"Who is he?" I said. "Any guess how long he'd been lying there?"

"There was no identification, and none of the nurses know him, so he's probably not local. We were sort of hoping you might know who he is."

"No clue," I said.

Something tugged at my brain, making me wonder what kind of kid comes to town and walks around with no wallet, no cell phone, no money in his pockets—but has the sharpest knife I'd ever seen. I could always take it down to the P.D., and have the locals lift his prints. If he had a police record, I'd be doing them a favor. On the other hand, I didn't want to buddy up to the local police if I didn't have to. A little town like this, they probably have plenty of time on their hands. If some over-achiever gets a bug up his butt and begins checking too deeply into my background he might find some inconsistencies.

Dr. Carstairs said, "As to how long he'd been lying on the ant hill, I'd have to say not very, because anaphylaxis occurs rapidly, within seconds to a minute. If I had to venture a guess, I'd say two, three minutes, tops."

Rachel said, "That poor kid must have been walking up from the beach when he got stung."

I said, "I think you're right. He was probably walking up from the beach and saw the car full of jerks heading in his direction, got scared, and ducked down for cover. Then the ants got him."

"Poor kid," she said. "Alone and scared."

"Yeah," I said.

But with a hell of a dangerous knife.

6.

NEXT MORNING I checked Rachel's pulse, kissed her on the cheek, and climbed out of bed. I left her a note to say I'd be back in time for the eight-thirty breakfast, then I put on some shorts and running shoes and hit the road.

With a four-thousand-year-old history rich with ancient Indians, marauding pirates, seafaring captains, railroads, shrimpers, saloons and sharks, St. Alban's, Florida, is a visitor's paradise.

I headed north on A1A and turned left on Coastal, followed Coastal all the way to the tiny airport that served Amelia Island, turned left again on Farthing, and wound up back on A1A, a couple miles south of the Seaside. Six minutes later I passed the area where we had our run-in with the homeboys and then the place where we saved the kid. I sprinted a half mile, then slowed to a cooling jog and stopped a few yards shy of the Seaside's front gate. The owner, Beth Daniels, was pulling weeds from the stone path that led to the front door.

"Enjoy your run?" she said, greeting me with a smile.

"Very much so."

Beth was fortyish, recently widowed, disarmingly attractive. She and her husband were said to have had legendary personalities, but she'd been in a deep funk these past months, consumed by the effort required to keep her husband's bed and breakfast dream alive. Charles had gone to Atlanta on business, suffered a heart attack, died within minutes, leaving Beth deeply in debt. Within weeks of his untimely death, she'd lost her cook, her waitress, and her caretaker. She had only one staff member left, a part-time cleaning lady.

"One thing I noticed while running," I said. "In store front windows, on telephone poles, and even a billboard: posters about the girl who went missing last year."

Beth nodded. "Libby Vail."

"What I was wondering, the posters say she went missing in Pennsylvania."

"That's my understanding."

"So why place them here in Florida?"

Beth dabbed at the light sweat on her face and forehead with the back of her garden gloves. "When it first happened, the police interviewed Libby's college room-mate. She told them Libby always talked about coming to St. Alban's to research her family tree."

"Did the cops trace her here?"

"No, she just seemed to disappear off the face of the earth. But when the story came out about her wanting to come here, the whole town got involved. We held candle-light vigils, and her parents came down and made some appeals on TV. Even the FBI set up a command post for a few days, but nothing came of it. Still, the town embraced the story, and every month since her disappearance, we've held a weekend celebration in Libby's honor."

"Celebration?"

"Like a festival. People come from all over the country. Some folks have come all the way from Europe."

"But your bed and breakfast isn't benefitting from all the business?"

"It's the only thing that's kept us going this long," Beth

said. "The whole town, for that matter. But with the economy the way it is, Charles had some investments in Atlanta that went bad, and we mortgaged this place to the roofline. Now interest rates are up and we're struggling to keep it going."

I glanced at the parking area. She followed my gaze and said, "Oh, I should have said something. Rachel left about thirty minutes ago. She took the car."

"She say where she was heading?"

"No. Sorry."

I waved my hand in the direction of the parking area. "The other guests?"

Beth sighed. "Gone."

"They left before breakfast?"

"You haven't had the privilege of tasting my cooking," she said. "If you had, you'd understand."

I smiled. "Surely you're kidding. Breakfast is easy."

She pursed her lips and made an expression that would have been adorable, had she not seemed so sad. She looked uncertain, as if she wanted to say something, but was trying to work up the courage.

"I don't suppose you want the chef's job?" She looked at me like a woman seeking space on an overcrowded lifeboat.

I could only think of two things in life worse than being a cook at a B&B in St. Alban's Beach, Florida.

"I need a caretaker, too," she said.

Being a caretaker was one of them.

"And a waitress."

That was the other.

I looked at the six-hundred-year-old live oaks surrounding the place.

"You're overrun with squirrels," I said.

"The one problem Charles was never able to solve," she

34

said. "Now we're about to implode from them. Do you have any suggestions?"

"The branches are giving them access. They've worked their way into the eaves. Your attic is crawling with them."

"You've heard them?"

"I have."

"I'm so sorry," she said. "In better times I'd offer you a refund."

I held up my hand. "Not necessary."

She smiled again. "You're very kind."

I motioned to the porch. "Let's sit a minute."

She cocked her head slightly, as if trying to decode my meaning.

I ignored her expression and climbed the steps and sat down facing her. Beth stood her ground.

"What are you up to, Mr. Creed?"

"I'm thinking about your offer."

"You're joking."

"Probably."

She moved closer. "You'd consider it?"

"I *am* considering it."

We were quiet a moment. I must have had a curious expression on my face because she said, "What on earth are you thinking?"

I laughed. "I'm trying to picture Rachel as a waitress."

Beth shared my laugh. She climbed the steps and sat beside me, then thought better of it, and scooted her bottom a proper distance away, just beyond the top of the steps. She allowed her legs to dangle off the porch, and removed her gloves.

She said, "It's easier picturing Rachel as a waitress than you as a cook."

"A cook and maintenance man," I said.

"That too," she said.

She laughed some more, and let it fade into a chuckle, and then we were silent again. She seemed to be regarding me in a different way, and I could feel her eyes studying my profile. When I turned toward her she quickly lowered her eyes.

"I can't pay much," she said.

"How bad are things with the bank?"

Her eyes began to well up. She bit her lip. "I'm on my last gasp."

I stood. "Give me a couple minutes."

I walked down the steps and circled the house, checking the foundation. I studied the overhang of the roof long enough to find two places where squirrels were getting into the attic. There were probably others. The thing about squirrels, they attract other pests, like mice and snakes. Who knew what might be living in that old attic?

The Seaside had a private wooden walkway that I followed down to the beach. The footboards were okay, but the handrails needed replacing. At the end of the walkway, there was a charming sitting area with two benches. Just beyond, a dozen steps led to the type of hard-packed sand you find on Atlantic coast beaches.

Today the sea action was moderate. Frothy waves tumbled onto the shore, dumping tiny white coquina shells that wiggled their way into the wet sand. I heard a noise, looked up, and saw a group of seagulls traveling a straight line just beyond the surf, scanning the waves like supermarket shoppers checking the shelves for their favorite food items.

A sudden gust kicked up from the beach. I closed my eyes and inhaled the salty scent. When I opened them I noticed what might have been sea turtle tracks leading from a nearby sand dune to the water. I viewed the B&B from the back.

It was a gorgeous old home, probably the nicest bed and breakfast I'd ever seen. But a proper restoration would require a serious injection of cash. I wondered if the place could ever turn a profit and decided the answer was no. Nevertheless, I found myself drawn to stay there and do what I could to help. It was almost as though the old home had singled me out and expected me to report to duty. And there was something else. That feeling of serenity I'd experienced the first night back. It seemed to have come with the sudden breeze off the water. I looked around to see if anything had recently entered my space: a bird, a bit of Spanish moss, some insects...but nothing seemed out of place. I turned back to the beach, but there were no answers to be found, in fact the beach was deserted, save for two women in big hats, wading in the far distance. I watched them walking away for a few moments, and suddenly the feeling was gone. I searched again for any clue that something was moving out of my immediate space, but all I came up with was that the wind had died down. I looked out to sea a minute, waiting for another gust. When it came, there was no feeling of serenity with it.

Perhaps I was going mad. Maybe Rachel's insanity was contagious.

I walked back to the front yard and found Beth where I'd left her.

"I'll do it," I said.

"You will?"

"Subject to Rachel's okay."

Beth's eyes lit up. "Really?"

I nodded.

"I don't believe it!" she said. "Thank you!"

She started to cry, softly. I wanted to hold her, tell her everything was going to be all right, but I'd just moved from

37

client to employee, and it wouldn't be proper. I stood there, feeling as useless as tits on a rooster, till she got herself together.

"I'm so sorry," she said.

"It's okay."

"I'm such a baby."

"You're doing the best you can, in a tough situation."

She nodded. "Can I ask you something about your decision to stay here?"

"Sure."

"Do you feel drawn to…to The Seaside in some manner?"

I studied her a moment. "How did you know?"

Suddenly she seemed younger, almost girlish.

"Can you really cook?" she said.

"Does it matter?"

7.

RACHEL WAS BACK. I didn't ask her where she'd been, and she didn't offer any explanation.

"You want me to be a waitress?" she said.

"Beth needs us," I said.

"Beth, huh?"

"Yup."

"She's pretty," Rachel said.

"You think?"

"You *know* she is. Should I be worried?"

"Not for a minute."

"Just so you know," she said. "If I ever catch you cheating, I'll cut your dick off and feed it to a seagull."

"It would have to be a helluva big seagull," I said.

"In your dreams!"

I frowned.

"Maybe I'll just toss it in the air and let a flock of seagulls fight over it," she said.

I winced at the visual.

"How long are we gonna do this?" she said.

"As long as it's fun for you."

"And the minute it's not?"

"We'll head to South Beach."

"Will you wear a big white chef's hat, like Chef Boyardee?"

"Not even to save my life," I said.

"In that case, I'll do it!"

Moments later she was telling Beth, "If I ever catch you fucking Kevin, I'll burn you up in your bed."

Beth gave me a look of horror and said, "Maybe this wasn't such a good idea."

"Kevin is a gourmet cook," Rachel said.

I shrugged.

"Rachel," Beth said, "I'm about to go broke. Every nickel I own is tied up in this place. I loved—and still love—my husband. I have no interest in developing a romantic relationship with—"

She looked at me. "Is it Donovan or Kevin?"

I shrugged again.

She continued. "Charles loved this place, it was his dream. It's all I have left of the man I loved with all my heart. But Rachel?"

Rachel looked at her.

"—I don't want to have to worry that every time Kevin and I are in the same room you're going to think something's up."

"I'm only concerned about the fucking," Rachel said.

"Then you've got nothing to worry about," Beth said.

Rachel threw her arms around Beth and said, "I love you, Beth. And you'll see, I'm going to be the best waitress you ever had!"

Beth looked at me wide-eyed and mouthed the words, "Is she crazy?"

I mouthed back, "She loves you."

8.

BOB POCKET WAS a normal-sized man with an enormous round belly. Sitting in his high-backed banker's chair, it looked like he was trying to hide a basketball under his shirt. He drummed his fingers on it, and I wondered if it was as solid as it appeared. It was truly amazing, and I couldn't wait to tell Rachel about it.

"Excuse me?" he said. "You're the what?"

"Chief cook and handyman."

"Well, Mr.—"

"Creed."

"Creed." He started to sneer, then caught himself and turned it into a broad smile. "It's wonderful to have you here, you're going to love our little town. All the people are amazing, the weather's amazing, the beach is wonderful, and like I say, the people are—"

"—Amazing," I said. "I get it."

Bob Pocket seemed about to frown, but again, he found a way to show me a pleasant, though unconvincing, smile. "I'm really not at liberty to discuss Ms. Daniels' financial affairs with her employees. I hope you can try to understand that."

I passed him a notarized power of attorney. He studied it carefully before saying, "She's way behind, but we haven't begun the foreclosure proceedings yet."

"Why not?"

"Well, this is hard to explain to an outsider, but our little town has a way of attracting good luck. Good things happen here, things that can't be explained. We're just trusting that something wonderful will happen, and Beth won't have to lose her special inn. Wait, why are you laughing?"

"You'll have to excuse me," I said. "I've never encountered a benevolent banker before."

Bob Pocket chuckled. "Benevolent banker," he repeated. "I like that. I guess we are a trusting bank, with an optimistic board of directors. But after you've been here awhile it will make more sense to you. This community has been blessed, and it's astounding how much good fortune we've attracted lately."

"The luck of St. Alban's?"

"You've heard about it?"

"Dr. Carstairs used the phrase."

Pocket nodded. "Good man. We're fortunate to have him with us."

"He's new to the town?"

"Came here a year ago, out of the blue, right when we needed him the most."

"Uh huh. So you're what, hoping another miracle will occur, and this time Beth's B&B will be saved?"

"I wouldn't say miracle, but yes, I suppose we tend to rely on some sort of cosmic balance. We've had bad times in the past, and now it's time for a rebirth. All the signs are pointing to a happy, prosperous community. Beth has had her troubles, but she's due for some good fortune. She's an asset to the community and she's got a charming little business, and we're just hoping for the best. Maybe your arrival has signaled the start of her good fortune."

"How much time does she have?" I asked.

He shook his head. "Board meeting's next Tuesday." He paused, and broke into a wide-faced grin. "But even if something wonderful doesn't happen by then, I'm sure Beth will recover. Things have a way of working out in our wonderful town. Beth will be happy and prosperous again, you'll see."

"How much does she owe?"

"The total note is a million-six," he said, "give or take."

Beth had an interest only note that ran about eight thousand a month. I knew she and Charles hadn't made any principal payments in more than a year. I also knew she was six months behind on her note.

Bob Pocket looked over the top of his reading glasses. "Perhaps you should consider finding employment elsewhere until things work out for Beth. There are golden opportunities everywhere, within the city limits."

I handed him a check for sixty thousand dollars.

"This should catch Beth up and take care of next month's payment," I said.

He studied the check as if it held a secret code. "This any good?" he asked.

"Call it in."

"Count on it."

"This check," I said.

"What about it?"

"This is between you and me. St. Alban's is a small town. I don't want anyone to know about this. Not even Beth."

"If the check is valid, Ms. Daniels will see it on her bank statement."

"By then it will be okay. In the meantime, I'm counting on your discretion."

"I'm just one part of the group," he said. "There are a

number of local board members who will learn about it."

"I don't want any talk."

"I can't speak for the whole town," he said. "But I can assure you, no one will question it." He stood, took my hand and pumped it vigorously. "You see? It's just as I've said. Every day something seems to happen that can't be explained. This town attracts good fortune. Has, ever since—"

I looked at him.

He shrugged. "Well, quite a while now. We like to think of it as our turn." He turned somber a moment. "We had a long dry spell. You can't imagine."

Pocket stared off into space. I came prepared to hear him ask if Beth and I were dating, but the possibility never seemed to cross his mind, which impressed me. Surely he wondered why I'd take a cook and caretaking job if I had this type of money. I had two reasons, but planned to keep a lid on them. First, I thought the structure of the job would help stabilize Rachel's mood swings, and second, I wanted to poke around to see if I could find the source of the power I'd felt twice in this strange little town. Something was drawing me to stay in St. Alban's, and if the townspeople were going to be seeing a lot of me, it made sense to have a reason for being here. Like a job. After a while Pocket seemed to remember he had company.

"I'm sorry," he said. "What was I saying?"

"You were saying I couldn't imagine the dry spell St. Alban's has had."

"Oh, right. Well, to be honest, I can't really imagine it, either. But I've heard the stories, we all have. During the worst of it, our forefathers barely managed to keep their families alive."

"Why's that?"

"The town was cursed."

"Excuse me?"

His words had come too quickly, and he seemed to regret having said them. He hastened to add, "But that was then, and this is now."

"The town was cursed?"

He smiled. "Forget I said that, it's just an old wives' tale, a figure of speech. What's important is the tide has turned, and it's a new day, a happy time for our town."

Pocket sat back in his chair and filled the silence between us by drumming his fingers on his belly. Before long he had a rhythm going where each tap produced a hollow sound not unlike a housewife thumping a melon for ripeness. He abruptly brought his concert to a close and looked at the check again.

"This is valid?" he said.

I nodded.

"And you're a cook."

"Cook and caretaker," I said.

He winked. "Amazing, isn't it?"

"What's that?"

"We've been holding off this foreclosure for six months, hoping something would work out. We're days away from filing, and suddenly, out of the blue, you and your girlfriend just happen to show up in time to save Beth's inn."

"So?"

"Don't you find that amazing? I mean, you being a total stranger and all?"

"I'm just protecting my job," I said.

I FIGURED BOB Pocket would be on the phone before I got out the front door. I also figured he'd shit his pants when he found out I could buy not only the bank in which he worked, but the whole town as well. I'd been worth a half-billion dollars before my recent score, but now my net worth was north of six billion. What could this tiny bank be worth, twenty million at best?

Two weeks ago I put twenty-five million in Rachel's account, which meant The Seaside's *waitress* could buy Pocket's bank. So yes, the check was good.

I walked across the street to Rider's Drug Store and purchased three EpiPens, which cut their supply in half. The pharmacist looked blissful. He said, "I just ordered those EpiPens last week."

"You sell a lot of them, do you?"

"In all the years I been here, I sold one," he said.

"That being the case, why'd you order six?"

"Just had a feelin'," he said.

"Got a feeling when you'll sell the other three?"

"Nope, but they'll sell before the expiration date, you can be sure of that."

I didn't know what gave him the confidence to make that statement, but a day ago I wouldn't have expected to buy three EpiPens, or even one, for that matter. Nor would I have imagined myself giving an innkeeper's banker a check for sixty grand. Maybe Bob Pocket was right. Maybe there was something charmed about this town. I just hoped the cosmic balance didn't depend on me.

I took a different route back to the Seaside, but I don't know why. Main Street to A1A would have been a clear shot, but for some reason High Street to Eighth felt more inviting. Maybe I was subconsciously trying to get the feel of the little town.

Something happened when I turned on High Street.

I felt a tingling sensation. A good one, like the kind you feel when you first climb under the covers on a cold night. The further I drove the more soothing it felt. By the time I hit Eighth, I was practically euphoric. This was the feeling I'd had two nights earlier, when I'd followed Rachel down A1A, and again yesterday when I stood behind the B&B, contemplating the caretaker's job. I drove past an empty tailor's shop, some old houses, and a boarded-up dry-cleaning store. At the intersection to A1A, on the left-hand corner, I saw a lady carrying what looked like a picnic basket up the steps of an old church. I remained there a moment, my eyes transfixed on the church. I'm not a religious man, nor even a spiritual one, but the feeling I was enjoying seemed to come from the area of the church.

I wasn't alone in this, either.

In the churchyard, standing reverently, but still, like statues, were half a dozen elderly people. Their eyes were turned skyward, or perhaps I should say balcony-ward, since the second-floor balcony on the side of the church seemed to be their point of focus. As I sat on my brake at the stop sign I noticed a small line of people turning the corner. They weren't together, and none were speaking. But all were making their

47

way toward the churchyard. There was also a van parked twenty yards to the side with two guys in the front seat. Like me, they appeared to be watching the statue people in the churchyard. They had almost certainly brought the first group of old people to the church and appeared to be waiting for them. I backed my rental car, turned into somebody's driveway, put my flashers on, and climbed out. Crossing the street, I approached two elderly women and a man bent over a cane.

"What's the attraction?" I asked.

No one answered.

Suddenly, one of the ladies sighed deeply and started moving her head around. Tears welled in her eyes and began streaming down her face. She rounded her shoulders as if warming up to take an exercise class. About that time the man's cane fell to the ground and he slowly straightened his back. A look of ecstasy crossed his face and tears flowed freely from his eyes. The third woman broke into a wide smile and started dancing in a tight little circle of space.

I looked around.

The others were making small movements with their bodies. Some of the new arrivals stood stock still, as if waiting for something marvelous to happen. Their eyes were hopeful and glazed over as if experiencing the type of rapture that comes from contemplating divine things. As I watched their faces break into euphoric smiles I was reminded of a tent show I'd been to as a kid, where a preacher offered to trade the town folk miracles for money.

Only there were no preachers around.

I didn't want to leave. But apparently the guys in the van had seen me trying to talk to the old folks, because the driver climbed out holding a cell phone to his ear, and within seconds, a cop car pulled in front of the church. I waved goodbye to my elderly friends and to the cops and van guys as well, and jogged back to my car. No sense in ruffling feathers my first day on the job.

I glanced at the church again and saw more people heading there. All were old or sickly, though some were being pushed in wheelchairs by younger, healthy people. All of them: healthy or sick, young or old, looked like they came for a miracle. Silently, I wished them well, but couldn't help thinking they were the same people who'd travel 50 miles and stand in line to see a piece of French toast that looks like St. Paul's bullfrog.

I backed onto Eighth, made my way to the corner and turned right on A1A. I'd got about a mile before losing the feeling of euphoria. I didn't know what the power was, or how it spread, but it seemed to emanate from the church. At least today it did. Of course, yesterday I felt it behind the B&B and the night before it occurred a mile further south. So what had I really learned? My life had been filled with strange experiences, but this one took the cake! If the town wanted to make a killing, maybe they could find a way to harness the energy around that church and sell it. I doubted that was possible, but on the chance it might be, I gave serious thought to heading back that way with an empty bottle and a cork.

But that would have to wait.

I drove another half-mile and turned into the parking lot of The Seaside B&B, where, as caretaker, my first order of business was squirrel infestation.

I'd begun my military career right out of high school as a sniper for the Army. In those days I learned how to move stealthily through the woods and tall grass, where distance traveled was often measured in feet per hour. What I'm saying, it was a rare day that I didn't encounter snakes, rodents and insects of all types, so I had no fear of St. Alban's tree squirrels.

But I had no intention of climbing into that attic yet.

Most animals will give you a wide berth, provided you don't back them in a corner. In the wild, there are plenty of escape routes for the big and small beasties, all of whom are nervous, frightened, or curious. When they see or hear or feel you coming, the nervous move on, the frightened growl or hiss and move on, and the curious stop to look, maybe piss or defecate near you, but eventually slither or scurry away.

But the Seaside attic was self-contained, with walls, a floor and a ceiling and only a few small holes available to the beasties as escape routes. I had no idea what might be lurking in the eaves and insulation-filled floorboards of that attic, but there was one thing I did know: this was their attic, not mine. It had been theirs for a long time, and I wasn't going to change that in a day, or even a week.

I had a plan.

My plan involved the ladder I found in the storage shed that was located to the side and back of the property. It looked to be about twelve-feet tall, with an extension that would take it up to about twenty.

Beth had gone to Jacksonville for the day, and guests weren't scheduled to arrive until after four, so Rachel and I had the place to ourselves. My plan was to make a quick, pre-emptive strike against the squirrels by boxing them in. I'd let them sit there awhile, let them expend some energy trying to scratch their way out, then gas them with a pesticide bomb and assess their response. I gathered some metal flashing, nails and a hammer, and propped the ladder against the side of the house by the openings the squirrels were using to enter and exit the attic. I boarded up the holes I could find. Then I put the ladder and other materials away, changed into a pair of khaki shorts, and swung by the kitchen long enough to crush some ice cubes in a blender and roll them into a hand towel. Then I headed to the beach where Rachel was sunbathing.

"Hey Scatman," Rachel said.

"Scatman?"

"I looked it up on my laptop," she said. "Scatman Crothers played the part of the caretaker in *The Shining*. Dick Hallorann?"

You had to love this girl: two days earlier I'd told her about the Grady Twins, today she was giving it back to me. Rachel had on a black and white striped bikini and was lying on a chaise longue. She wore her hair in a French braid with a white bow tied on the end. She'd pulled the braid over her left shoulder to frame her face. The glass beside her was empty; save for a small pool of water and a couple of nearly melted ice cubes, remnants of what I guessed had been a pina colada.

"Where'd you get the drink?" I said.

"I made it in the kitchen. They don't have anyone to serve drinks here, can you believe that?"

"I think the waitress is supposed to serve the drinks."

She looked at me curiously. "Well, that's what I did."

I nodded.

Rachel said, "What's with the towel?"

"Here, I'll show you." I put the frozen towel around her neck.

She gasped when it touched her skin, but within seconds she was murmuring, "God, that feels good!"

I said, "I think I'll take the car down A1A for a few minutes."

"Like how many minutes?"

"Maybe twenty. You want to come?"

"No, I'm good. I want to catch some rays today if we're

still doing breakfast tomorrow. Are we?"

"We are."

She looked up at me and squinted against the sun. "You sure you want to do that? Cook breakfast for tourists and townies?"

"I am. Can I get you another drink before I go?"

"Maybe you could bring me one when you come back."

I kissed her on the cheek. "As you wish," I said, quoting a line from our favorite movie, *The Princess Bride*.

"Thank you, Farm Boy," Rachel said, not to be outdone.

A few minutes later I took A1A back to the church, but this time I felt nothing. Nor were there any old people in the churchyard. Whatever had happened, if it happened, had stopped happening. But I didn't care; I knew how to find another great feeling.

I turned the car around and headed to the sand dune where we'd found the boy a couple nights ago. I parked on the shoulder of the highway and made my way to the fire ant colony, and lay on my back next to it the same way the kid had been laying. While I waited I wondered what I'd tell the cops if a squad car happened by.

Within minutes I felt them crawling on my arms and legs.

I closed my eyes and smiled.

10.

D'AUGIE HAD BEEN surprised to see Rachel sitting at the foot of his hospital bed the morning after his fire ant incident. She'd come to check on him, she said, adding that she and Kevin had come the night before for the same purpose. She'd laughed when he told her his name, and barked a couple of times. Under normal circumstances, he'd have slit a woman's throat for making fun of him, but with Rachel, it seemed so childlike and cute, he found himself laughing along with her.

"Is it spelled D-O-G-G-Y?"

He told her the correct spelling.

"Is it foreign?"

D'Augie changed the subject. "Did you happen to find my knife last night?"

"You had a knife?"

"More like a pocket knife," he lied.

So Creed must have found the knife and kept that information from Rachel. Which meant he'd be suspicious, and have his guard up next time D'Augie attacked. D'Augie had been mortified to hear that Creed saved his life. But it didn't change things. He still intended to kill him, first chance he got. He decided to play it cool with Rachel, see if he could get some information that would help him kill her boyfriend.

He watched her remove a plastic water bottle from her purse and shake it. Then she unscrewed the cap, poured something red and gloppy from it into a plastic cup on his hospital table, and handed it to him.

"What's this?" he said.

"Red Drink."

"What's in it?"

"Water, grape juice, pomegranate juice, cranberry juice, protein powder, birch bark, a bit of citrus, some other stuff."

He held it up to the light and stared at it. "What's it for?"

"It's full of antioxidants, and prevents you from getting sick. But if you're already sick or get hurt, it heals you quickly."

"This some sort of family potion?"

"No, it's Kevin's recipe."

D'Augie abruptly put the cup down and silently cursed himself for being so stupid. He must have been reeling from the effect of the drugs they'd given him to have considered drinking this red concoction in the first place. He looked at the puzzled expression on her face. Then again, if Creed wanted to kill him, he'd already be dead. He wouldn't have sent this girl to poison him.

"What's wrong?" Rachel said.

Unless she was one of Creed's assassins.

"D'Augie?"

But if she was one of his assassins, would she be so stupid as to tell him the drink was Creed's recipe?

D'Augie looked her over carefully, while thinking about the events from the night before, the events prior to landing on the fire ant hill. Such as watching Creed and Rachel at dinner, their tender scene on the porch, and the way she stomped off into the night cursing like a sailor. D'Augie had seen women act like that before, but they weren't assassins. They were angry girlfriends.

"Kevin told you to give this to me?"

Rachel laughed. "No, silly. I made it. It's Kevin's recipe, but I make it for him all the time."

D'Augie looked at the liquid in cup. "You ever try it?"

"We drink it almost every morning. It's really good for you. I wouldn't have brought it if it wasn't."

"Show me," he said.

"What?"

He handed her the cup. "Show me how good it tastes."

Rachel took it and shrugged. "Seriously?"

"Unless there's some reason you'd rather not."

Rachel made a face that would have been adorable had she not been trying to poison him. Then, to D'Augie's surprise, she drank half the cup, paused, then placed the cup carefully on the table and smiled.

"See?" she said. "Delicious, nutritious, and healthy." She suddenly made a face, grabbed her throat and said, "Wha... what...Oh, my God, I...I don't feel so good...I—" then she fell to the floor.

D'Augie jerked himself to a sitting position and peered over the edge of the bed. Rachel jumped up, yelled "Boo!" and nearly scared the shit out of him.

"Sorry," Rachel said, "but you deserved that."

She seemed to study his face a moment. "You're pale," she said. "Hey, I didn't mean to frighten you. Are you okay?"

He nodded.

Rachel moved around the side of the bed and, to D'Augie's utter amazement, she kissed his forehead. Then she stroked his hair a moment before reclaiming her seat. She picked up the cup and drank some more and said, "You sure you don't want some? I've got..." She looked at the plastic bottle on the hospital table. "Half a bottle left. You want to watch me drink that too?"

"I'll split it with you."

D'Augie drank while Rachel talked. She told him that she and Creed were on vacation, and had traveled the eastern sea coast for two weeks. That wasn't news to D'Augie, since he'd been hunting Creed for months, showing his photo to all the private jet operators and airports around the country. A couple of weeks ago a Louisville baggage guy remembered a man who fit Creed's physical description, who had demanded strict secrecy. But he said the man used a different name and the photo was all wrong. The guy he'd seen looked like a movie star and didn't have a jagged scar on the side of his face. D'Augie decided Creed must have changed his appearance. He'd heard Homeland Security assassins could do that, but D'Augie's informant gave him a critical piece of information: the guy who might be Creed was traveling with a young lady named Rachel Case. So regardless of the name Creed was using on the manifest, Rachel was using her real name, and they had left Louisville for Atlantic City a few days earlier. D'Augie had googled Rachel Case, from Louisville, found her photos, learned her background information. Then he scoped out the nicest hotels in Atlantic City until he saw Rachel lounging at the pool drinking Kashenkas with a guy that had to be Donovan Creed. Sure enough, when he called the front desk, they confirmed a Donovan Creed was registered there.

So D'Augie began following them, and had followed them ever since.

As Rachel talked, D'Augie allowed himself to wonder if the "Red Drink" could be one of Creed's secret weapons. He'd heard all his life about how Creed seemed impervious to pain, and how he had a miraculous ability to heal after receiving the most savage blows and wounds. His father had known Creed, and had considered him to be superhuman. D'Augie had always assumed Creed's mysterious powers were more hyperbole than fact. But after drinking this red concoction, he was beginning to change his mind. There was no arguing the way this drink made him feel. He was gaining strength and energy. He was getting better.

"Rachel," he said, "This Red Drink is to die for!"

"I told you you'd love it!"

They spent the next fifteen minutes chatting about fire ants (neither liked them) and how D'Augie was feeling (much better, thank you). The doctors said he might be able to get out in a couple of weeks, but if she brought him some more Red Drink it might only take a couple of days, he speculated. She agreed to come back the next day.

Rachel wasn't what D'Augie would call smokin' hot, but she had plenty going for her. High on the list, she seemed to care what happened to D'Augie, which was something he wasn't used to. He wouldn't feel the slightest regret for killing Creed, but he decided he would spare Rachel's life, if at all possible.

The next morning, Thursday, Rachel brought him two bottles of Red Drink and a book. Even better, she told him that she and Creed had taken jobs at The Seaside to help out the lady who owned the place. Rachel laughed at the idea she was going to be a waitress. D'Augie laughed at the idea Creed was going to start cooking breakfast for the guests. They spoke a bit more, and then Rachel said, "I guess I better head out."

"Why the rush?"

"I'm going to catch some rays on the beach."

"With Kevin?"

"I wish! No, Kevin's going to start getting rid of the tree

squirrels today."

"Tree squirrels?"

"In the attic. At The Seaside."

She rambled on about how the squirrels had nested in the attic and were making noises, and how Kevin had decided not to climb up there for a few more days, and…

…And that's how D'Augie figured out how to kill Creed without hurting Rachel.

Ninety minutes after Rachel left, D'Augie finished his second bottle of Red Drink, grabbed his clothes and snuck out of the Medical Center. He walked to the public parking area on Front Street where he'd left his car before following Creed and Rachel down A1A a couple nights earlier. He retrieved a shirt and hat from the trunk and put them on, then drove to a supermarket and bought some peanut butter meal replacement bars, a half-dozen bottles of water, and a boning knife. He put these items and a 9mm Glock in a small carry bag in his trunk and drove to the public beach parking lot. He parked his car, got the carry bag from the trunk and slung it over his shoulder. Then he walked the beach a quarter-mile until he saw Rachel fifty yards in front of him, lying on a chaise longue.

He paused for a moment to look at her. Rachel's body looked better in the bikini than he'd thought it would a few hours earlier, when she'd come to visit him in the hospital. He allowed himself to imagine her naked. From there it was a short hop to think about making love to her, and he wondered if, after killing Creed, he should contact her and help her get through the grieving stage. After a suitable period of being her emotional tampon, D'Augie could make his move.

Speaking of moves, it was time to decide his next one. D'Augie shook the image of naked, grieving Rachel from his mind and glanced behind her, intending to check out the rear entrance to The Seaside. But what he saw instead was Creed walking on the boardwalk, coming from the B&B, heading toward Rachel, carrying a wrapped-up towel.

D'Augie abruptly turned toward A1A, climbed over some sand dunes and slogged his way a hundred yards through shifting sand until he got to the highway. He propped himself against a telephone pole that had a poster nailed to it. He looked at the picture and skimmed the words about a missing girl named Libby Vail. From this position he had a clear view of the side and back of The Seaside. After a few minutes he saw Creed heading back. Then he was out of view for a moment. Then he reappeared in the parking lot, where he got in a car and drove away.

Moments later, D'Augie entered The Seaside, calling out, "Is anyone here?" If someone had answered, he'd ask for a brochure and leave. But he knew there was no one inside because he counted four mice running around on the main floor, and a wharf rat. Rachel had told him that Creed planned to board up the attic, so he'd probably already done it and the rodents were fleeing through interior openings and floorboards.

He headed up the stairs and located the attic entrance in the ceiling above the hallway. He pulled the draw cord that opened the attic door, unhinged the attic steps, pulled them to the floor, and then tested them. Then he reversed the process and closed the attic and checked the floor to make sure there were no tell-tale signs on the carpet, like dust or insulation. Satisfied with the result, D'Augie opened the door again, lowered the stairs, and climbed into the attic.

11.

THE FIRE ANTS hurt like a son-of-a-bitch!

From the time I pulled the kid off the ant hill I'd been dying to experience the sensation. Don't get me wrong, I didn't plan to get swarmed like the kid, but I figured a couple dozen or so would give me the buzz I'd been missing these past weeks. Though I had an EpiPen in my pocket, I wasn't worried about anaphylactic shock, since Dr. Carstairs had said it's usually the second attack that gets you, not the first.

I let them feast on my flesh a few seconds before standing up and crushing them. A few got into my crotch and bit me hard enough to make my lower lip twitch. I figured to let the bites heal and come back every few days to see if I could build up a resistance.

By the time I got to the car I was feeling dizzy. It wouldn't take too many bites to go beyond the point of no return, so I made a mental note to be extra careful the next time. According to Dr. Carstairs, each exposure is exponentially more dangerous than the previous one.

I checked my watch; figured Rachel wouldn't care if I made a quick detour. I drove to the hardware store on Sixth and Coastal, got three feet in the door before the owner asked, "You the one taking over for Rip at The Seaside?"

"Was Rip the old caretaker?"

"Yep."

"Then, yep."

The owner was big and burly, with enormous fiery-red mutton chops that covered the entire space between his nose and lower lip. He wore a red flannel shirt with the sleeves rolled up to his elbows. Had a tattoo of a ship's anchor on one forearm, and a dancing girl on the other. Wore his pants low, beneath his beer belly, with no belt. He sized me up. "You don't look much like a caretaker, you don't mind me saying so."

"I'm more of a cook with a squirrel problem."

"You guys serve squirrel over there? Fried squirrel, milk gravy?"

The assistant manager sauntered over. He was tall and gaunt, with facial skin so leathery you could strop a razor on it. He wore a patch on his work shirt that told anyone who cared that he was Earl. It had been quite a while since I'd seen anyone saunter, and I took a minute to watch him. It's kind of a lost art and Earl was good at it.

"Let's start over," I said. I put out my hand. "I'm Donovan Creed."

The big man took it. "I'm Jimbo Pim, this here's Earl Stout."

I nodded at Earl and concluded the handshake and said, "I'm the caretaker and breakfast chef at The Seaside. I've got the breakfast part down, but I need some kind of bomb or spray to kill the squirrels and other varmints in the attic."

Jimbo rubbed his beard in a practiced manner with his thumb and index finger.

"Is Beth planning to shut the place down a few weeks?"

"No."

"Then I'd recommend against the bomb. Puts one hell of a sulfur stink in the air, takes about two weeks to get 'er gone. Not only that, but sprays and mothballs and the like can cause breathing problems for your customers."

"In that case, what do you recommend?"

"You been up in that attic?"

"Not yet."

"Then you don't know what the hell's up there. Them live oak branches hang way over the roof. You could have five species of snakes in there, maybe some raccoons to boot. The bomb and spray don't work on all critters. You kill the snakes you'll be overrun with rats. You kill the rats, the snakes will work their way into the living areas, and nothin' says 'leave' faster than snakes on a doorknob."

"Is that a local saying?"

"It should be. A few years back I found a corn snake wrapped around my bedroom doorknob."

He waited for me to ask about it, and I was convinced nothing would happen until I did.

"What did you do?" I said.

"Stuffed him in a shoebox, put a Bible on it and took him to the woods the next day."

"You weren't worried he'd get out in the middle of the night?"

"Snakes don't mess with The Word."

I looked at Earl. He nodded and said, "Goes back to Adam and Eve."

"Something else," Jimbo said. "It's against Florida law to kill tree squirrels."

Thinking Jimbo might be having sport with me, I looked at Earl again. But Earl nodded solemnly, so either they were both joshin' or they shared the same opinion about the killing of squirrels.

"But, they're basically rodents, right?"

"In Florida they're game mammals," Jimbo said, "so

they're protected under state hunting regulations."

I shook my head.

Earl said, "I know. What's the world coming to, right?"

"Any legal way around it?"

"Squirrels chew wires," Jimbo said. "They're a major fire hazard. You're probably close to a serious problem already, so you could go to a state wildlife damage control agent and apply for a depredation permit."

I frowned. "That sounds lengthy. You got any quick and easy solutions? I'm not hung up so much on the legality."

"Have you discussed these plans with Beth?"

"She's turned the squirrel problem over to me. Getting rid of them had been her husband's pet project, the one he hadn't been able to solve, and I'd like to do this for her."

"She's a hell of a woman," Earl said. "Charlie was a lucky man."

Jimbo said, "It pains me to see her so broken-hearted. They had the perfect marriage, far as the rest of us could tell."

Earl added, "She used to laugh all the time. That's what she was known for, friendly smile, big laugh."

"Don't see her doing much of either these days," Jimbo said.

We fell silent a moment.

"The squirrels?" I said.

"Look," Jimbo said. "There's about five ways to get rid of squirrels in an attic. But none of them work."

I waited for him to make sense out of that ridiculous statement, but Jimbo just stared at me as though the conversation was over. I didn't know what to say, so I just said, "Why not?"

"Well, The Seaside ain't had a caretaker a while and there was a squirrel problem before that."

The more Jimbo talked, the less sense he made. I said, "I know squirrels and mice tend to inhabit the same areas, and snakes can dig in. But it seems to me if you board them up—"

"Oh *hell* no!" Jimbo shouted. "You don't *never* want to board up a bunch of squirrels!"

"Why not?"

Jimbo became animated, flapping his arms like a heron on a pond, trying to create lift. He wanted to respond, but couldn't seem to find the right words. Earl beat him to it.

"Pandemonium!" he said.

12.

I RACED BACK to The Seaside with every intention of changing my clothes, getting the ladder out, and removing the metal flashing so the squirrels and other critters could escape before pandemonium ensued.

But when I went up the stairs toward my room I realized pandemonium had come and gone.

The attic access door had been located in the ceiling above the upper hallway. Now there was a huge hole where the door had been. The attic stairs were still folded up, like they should be, but the access door was on the floor in splinters, and a snake with a crushed head lay on it. The snake looked to be about six feet long, and was likely a rat snake. Wood was splintered all over the carpeting and squirrels were running amok throughout the house.

I propped the front door open and herded the squirrels out the door as best I could. Along the way, I encountered three snakes of similar length, but no rats. I suspected the new guests and I would find some rats later that night.

Rachel's blood-curdling scream told me she'd found one of the snakes in the back hallway as she tried to enter the house. I raced down the steps for the fifth time in ten minutes and removed the snake from her view while explaining the situation. Rachel turned and ran, and I continued working until I was convinced the squirrels and snakes were out of the house.

I decided Jimbo and Earl were wrong about not boarding up the escape routes, because when I pulled down the attic ladder and climbed up into the attic, I found a few baby squirrels, twenty feet of soiled, feces-soaked insulation, and nothing more. I relocated the baby squirrels to the side yard and drove back to the hardware store to buy some plywood I could use to board up the hole until I could get a new door ordered.

Jimbo said, "I'll order you one, but we're talkin' six weeks, maybe longer. You just don't see many doors like that no more."

I also bought a can of paint that seemed a close match to the ceiling color, and figured I had just enough time to secure the plywood, spray paint it, and tidy things up before the guests checked in.

On the way back to The Seaside I started working on an explanation for Beth as to how five snakes and a dozen squirrels could crash through an attic door, and how one of the snakes had gotten crushed to death in the process.

13.

D'AUGIE HAD BEEN smart to bring bottles of water because the attic was stifling, like a sauna. It was pitch black inside, but when D'Augie had opened the attic door and climbed up the steps, there'd been enough light to take in the general layout. He'd seen there was no floor or furniture to sit on, just beams separated by insulation, which meant he'd have an uncomfortable wait until Creed returned.

No problem, D'Augie could handle discomfort. He was, in fact, a powerhouse of will, a rock of discipline. He'd handled the fire ant bites, hadn't he? He had underestimated the fire ant threat. In the future, he planned to give them a wide berth. But attic heat and squirrels? No problem. He'd been in saunas before, just as he'd spent time in parks feeding squirrels.

D'Augie sat a minute, felt the sweat accumulating in pools underneath his shirt and pants and realized there was a big difference between saunas and attic heat. For one thing he'd never worn clothes in a sauna. Nor had he spent time in a sauna with fire ant bites that hadn't completely healed. The cramped conditions and sweltering attic heat were having an effect on his bites. D'Augie's thighs and crotch were beginning to itch and sting.

No problem, D'Augie would just rub some ointment on the trouble spots. He'd thought ahead, swiped a tube of ointment from the hospital, put it in his shirt pocket a couple hours ago, and...

...and *shit!*

While the tube of ointment was still in his shirt pocket, he realized he'd left that particular shirt in the trunk of his car when he changed clothes and put on the ball cap. Was it the power of suggestion that made his itching worse? D'Augie hoped so, because if it were an issue of mind over matter he'd be fine. He knew his mental powers were second to none, thanks to the countless hours he'd invested over many months mastering the art of meditation. He'd studied with the best yogis and perfected the art.

D'Augie spent the next five minutes in a deep meditative state. He would have devoted even more time to the meditating, but his crotch was on fire. It hurt like hell and was getting worse. He unzipped the top of the carry bag on his shoulder, took out a bottle of water, twisted the cap, and took a long sip. Then he unzipped his pants and poured some water on his festering blisters.

D'Augie knew there were squirrels in the attic, so he had expected to encounter the scent of feces in the air. He'd been around feces before, had a cat he used to clean up after a few years back. But this attic stench beat anything he'd whiffed in his lifetime. It was unearthly, truly appalling. Made his eyes itch and water and triggered his gag reflex. This odor was rich in feces, but there was more going on here than simple squirrel shit. D'Augie was a city boy, so he couldn't be certain, but there seemed to be at least two other odors at work, fighting for dominance. He was pretty sure that the more pleasant of the two was rotting carcass, while the other might be something like undigested, regurgitated, decaying animal bits. Whatever the nature of the smell, it was harsh enough to scare a mongrel off a corn dog.

But...no problem, D'Augie would deal with it. He took another sip of water.

The attic insulation was the pink roll type with paper on top. He had been hearing intermittent scurrying sounds on the paper some distance in front of him, and—there, it happened again—behind him. The sounds were too light to be squirrels, too heavy to be mice. Large mice? Small rats?

Moments later D'Augie heard chattering sounds in one of the eaves that were probably baby squirrels. Though he had spent little time in the country, he knew that in the animal kingdom new mothers are often fiercely protective and rarely stray far from their litters. So he made a mental note to stay away from the eaves. That wouldn't be a problem, assuming Creed returned soon. But if he didn't, D'Augie would be forced to stand and walk around a bit to keep his muscles from cramping up. Nothing ruins the element of surprise like jumping through a plywood door and attacking Creed on your knees.

The itching and burning in his thighs and crotch had escalated far beyond anything D'Augie's meditation could handle. It felt like someone was repeatedly burning his nuts and thighs with miniature branding-irons. Bad as the stink in the attic was to deal with, the fire ant pain in his loins was worse. D'Augie scratched his crotch vigorously, and experienced instant relief.

For about five seconds.

Then the itching and burning returned, and when it did, it was worse than before. D'Augie clenched his fists, gritted his teeth, and handled the itch and burn for about twenty seconds. Then he gave in and scratched his crotch again. And again.

...And managed to scratch the scabs off his wounds.

He'd been sweating profusely since entering the attic, and

sweat contained salt, so D'Augie wasn't surprised that the sweat stung his private area when it seeped into his open sores.

What did surprise him was how badly it hurt.

He wondered why this attic attack seemed like such a great idea earlier in the day. Now he was dealing with itchy crotch, *burning* crotch, horrific smells, cramping muscles, rats, baby squirrels, and...

What was that?

More scurrying on paper, only much louder.

And then a thwack.

And then the muffled squeaking sound a rat might make if it had been crushed in the jaws of...

...Of a huge snake.

D'Augie felt the hairs on the back of his neck tingle, as if something cold were blowing on them. If that was a snake it was a large one, and very close by. And where there's one it's almost certain there'll be another. The attic was virtually pitch black. Snakes could be slithering all around him, and he would never know it. They could be surrounding him at that very moment.

D'Augie was a city boy, not a country one. But he wasn't completely clueless. He knew, for example, that most snakes are not venomous. But he didn't know how many were.

He tried to remain calm. He drained his bottled water and put the empty in his carry sack. Then he did something a country boy would never do: he suddenly introduced a fresh food source into an enclosed attic space where wild animals and reptiles were trapped, fearful, and starving to death. He removed a peanut butter meal replacement bar from his carry sack and tore off the wrapper, releasing the scent of peanuts and chocolate into the air. As he started to move the food toward his mouth, something happened that caused him to forget his itchy, burning crotch and all the rest of his attic problems.

The battle was over as quickly as it started. D'Augie screamed and leaped through the plywood door with a snake on his face and two squirrels biting various parts of his neck and shoulders all the way to the floor. His elbow landed on the snake's head, crushing it, and the squirrels panicked and ran through the house. Before D'Augie could get to his feet, a dozen more squirrels came pouring out of the opening like lemmings, followed by half as many snakes, representing several varieties. As the creatures landed on or around him, D'Augie scrambled to get to his feet.

But couldn't.

Along with the numerous cuts, scrapes, bites and bruises he'd acquired before and during the fall, he'd apparently broken an arm and leg at the end of it.

"This is bullshit!" he screamed, covering up and waiting for the last of the critters to stop raining down from the shattered plywood hole above him. When at last things had quieted down, D'Augie secured his shoulder bag and began the slow and painful process of getting himself down the stairs, out the door, and to his car a quarter-mile away.

14.

IT WAS FRIDAY morning, and Rachel was upstairs making herself pretty. I was in the kitchen, cooking up a storm for the guests, and Beth was setting the dining room tables. Wherever the rats and mice were hiding, it worked, because the two couples that checked in yesterday made it through the night without screaming.

"What is that heavenly scent?" Beth asked.

"I'm baking a caramel bread pudding custard."

She walked back into the kitchen and eyeballed me. "You're joking."

"Want to see it?"

I led her to the oven and opened the door and said, "You'll get the full aroma in about twenty minutes."

"You've made this before, right?"

"Let me put it this way: within a week people will travel from parts unknown just to eat breakfast here."

"If you cook as well as you brag, my troubles are over."

I put my hand on my heart and bowed. "No one can brag as well as I cook. Not even me."

She looked past me, to the box on the far counter. "What's this?"

"Fresh flowers for the centerpiece."

Beth used both hands to smooth her hair back. "Custard, fresh flowers. I'm not sure you realize how deeply in debt I am."

"Relax. It's my treat."

Rachel made her way down the steps treading lightly in black, espadrille wedge sandals. She wore pale-pink lipstick and had on a white dress shirt with a high button-down collar, and black stretch jeans. The jeans looked particularly hot. She carried a crystal vase that I knew to be Baccarat. Reacting to Beth's stunned expression, Rachel said, "For the centerpiece." She spied the box of flowers and opened it and began arranging them in the vase.

Beth hadn't moved a muscle since entering the kitchen. She continued staring at the vase. "Who *are* you people?" she said.

Rachel's lips curled into a smile that resembled a pretty pink bow. She winked at me, and I took the cue.

"We are people not to be trifled with," I said.

"Excuse me?"

Rachel said, "That's a line from our favorite movie, *The Princess Bride*."

"Oh," Beth said. "Well, if it's your favorite, I'll have to check it out."

"It's about a pirate," Rachel said. "We love pirates, don't we, Kevin?"

"Arrr," I said. "And them who likes 'em, too."

"And their ships and crew members," Rachel said.

"Aye, and their families as well," I said, getting into it.

"And don't forget their descendants," Rachel said.

"Aye, especially them—"

And then something creepy happened. Beth slowly turned toward Rachel, turned so slowly I thought she must be imitating a scene from her own favorite movie, except that her face had lost all color and expression. When at last Beth's eyes met Rachel's, she spoke in a voice so chilly it seemed to freeze the room.

"What's going on here?" she said. Then she looked at me.

I shrugged. "We're saving your bed and breakfast. I'm cooking, Rachel's serving."

Beth looked at us a long time, making up her mind about something. Whatever it was, it seemed to go in our favor because a bit of the color came back to her face and she managed a tight smile. "In that case," she said, "I'd better get out the trays and bowls and serving spoons."

She headed back into the dining room and busied herself in the hutch. Rachel and I exchanged a glance.

"What was *that* all about?" Rachel whispered.

"Hell if I know," I said. "*You're* the woman."

Rachel made a soft singing sound, "Doo doo doo doo," which I recognized as the theme from the *Twilight Zone*.

15.

THERE'S NO POINT in being modest: the guests loved my bread pudding. They also raved about my cream biscuits, sausage gravy, and the French toast I'd stuffed with apple pie filling. But it was the mini BLT rounds that made the guests delirious. I had punched circles out of sliced potato bread with a large biscuit cutter, filled them with bacon, fresh tomatoes and romaine lettuce. Of course, the bacon was distinctively prepared. I started with thick slices, pressed them in brown sugar, and broiled them in the oven over a drip pan. The result was elegant, unique, and tasty enough to make a jackrabbit jump up and slap a hound dog.

"Mr. Creed," one of the ladies said. "Wherever did you study food preparation?"

"Why, in Paris, of course!" Rachel gushed.

I hadn't done anything of the kind. I was, in fact, self-taught. But Rachel's lie set so well with the guests I didn't have the heart to correct her.

This morning she'd been charming and sweet, though I wondered how she'd react to a large crowd and long lines of hungry customers waiting to be seated.

I didn't need to worry: she had done an excellent job with the serving. She had a natural rhythm about her, an athletic grace that was evident in everything she did. I loved watching her move. She could be walking down a flight of stairs or

75

carrying platters in and out of a busy kitchen, it didn't matter.

She was, in my eyes, a work of art.

Over the next few days Rachel and I settled into our routines. Afternoons, she'd shop for groceries, and I sawed off tree limbs that overhung the roof. Word on our food had gotten out, and we were doing ten tables of breakfast with the locals, more than half our capacity. Beth hired a teenager, Tracy, to help Rachel with the waitressing duties. Bob Pocket, the banker, had become a regular, and even Jimbo and Earl showed up twice, though they were disappointed to find us fresh out of squirrel both times.

Thursday morning, after our last breakfast guest had been served, I noticed Beth packing leftovers into a picnic basket.

"Hot date?" I said.

She didn't look up. "Sick friend."

Though Beth had been pleasant all week, she'd never gotten back to the degree of friendly she'd been prior to Rachel's comment about the pirates. She added four bottles of water to the basket and headed out the door without elaborating further. But as I saw her step out the door with the basket, my mind flashed to the quaint little church I'd passed the previous week, and the lady I'd seen carrying a similar picnic basket up the church steps.

"Think she's got a fella?" Rachel said.

"Why would you jump to that conclusion?"

"Might explain why she's acting so weird."

Rachel was hand-washing the dishes before putting them in the dishwasher. A few strands of hair kept falling over one of her eyes. She straightened up, stuck her bottom lip out and tried to blow them off her face, but that didn't work. She tossed her head, but that didn't work either. She sighed, wiped her hands on her apron, and tucked the errant strands

76

behind her ear. Then she said, "Are you still happy doing this?"

She extended an arm when she said it, indicating the kitchen, but I knew what she meant. It was a lot of work, and not the type I'd done before, at least not exclusively. For more years than I care to remember, my days consisted of hunting people or trying to keep from being hunted. I had acquired—okay, stolen—billions of dollars from the world's wealthiest and most dangerous criminals. Rachel didn't know I was a paid assassin, but she knew I was pretty comfortable financially. She, herself, had become a multimillionaire through her association with me.

"We could be anywhere in the world right now," she said, "doing anything we've ever wanted to do."

"True."

"And?"

"It's been a nice break for me," I said.

"Just to be clear: if you could be anywhere in the world, doing anything you've ever wanted to do, this is what you'd choose?"

I glanced around the kitchen and back at her. "At this exact moment in time? Yes."

"Uh huh. And why's that?"

"For starters, I've always wanted to vacation with a beautiful girl."

"Not a gorgeous one, like me?"

"I meant to say gorgeous."

"A gorgeous girl like me that you love with all your heart."

"Exactly."

"But?"

"But I've also learned that I need to stay busy."

"You love to cook," she said.

"I do love to cook. But I wouldn't want to cook for a large restaurant, or have to prepare more than one meal a day. I also enjoy working with my hands, but I wouldn't want to be a full-time maintenance guy. This place," I gestured the way she had, "doesn't require too much cooking or maintenance. I get to hang out with you, and we've got the beach, the sun, the sand…"

"But there's something else."

I paused. "There is something else."

We looked at each other a minute and she said, "Are you going to tell me or do I have to beat it out of you?"

"I feel ridiculous saying it out loud, but…"

"But?"

"There's something going on in this town," I said, "some type of mysterious presence. A power that comes and goes."

"A power."

"Surely you've felt it."

"Jesus, Kevin. *I'm* supposed to be the crazy one."

I shrugged, thought about saying "You're still plenty crazy," but didn't.

She looked at me curiously. "It's almost like paradise to you, now that you've got these projects going."

"For now it is."

Rachel nodded, and went back to loading the dishwasher. "You're expecting a lot from me, after inviting me to go on a vacation with you," she said.

I let that comment hang in the air, and worked her entire conversation around in my mind as I scrubbed down the kitchen surfaces. The first two weeks of our coastal vacation had been right out of the millionaire's handbook, and Rachel had loved the five-star resorts in Virginia and Georgia, the limos, fancy restaurants, luxurious pools and spas.

Now that I thought about it, she hadn't been remotely enthused when I brought up the idea of hitting St. Alban's and checking out a quaint little B&B called The Seaside. But she agreed to come, and she did it for me. Then, a day into our stay, I'd thrown her into a waitressing job she wouldn't have tolerated under any other circumstances.

I thought about Rachel's comment, and what she'd asked me, and realized there were probably a hundred places she'd rather be right now. On the other hand, I couldn't help but notice her mental condition had improved dramatically since we'd come here. It seemed to change the moment we found that kid on the ant hill. Or maybe the moment just before, when we were exposed to the power for the first time.

"I never thought to check on that kid," I said.

"You mean Tracy?"

"No, I meant—"

"Where is she, anyway? I thought she was hired to help us clean. All she's doing is food service."

"Beth said she starts full-time on Monday."

"She's kind of creepy, don't you think?"

"Beth or Tracy?"

Rachel turned to face me. "Both. But this Tracy girl, I don't know. She's like a robot or something."

"You mean because she's always happy?"

"Exactly. She's too happy. You know that movie, *Stepford Wives*? She's Stepford happy. In fact, everyone in St. Alban's seems to have that sort of vacant happiness."

Rachel hadn't just hit it, she'd knocked it out of the park. I wondered if the collective happiness among the locals had anything to do with the strange feeling I'd experienced.

"I've noticed that," I said. "Everyone we've met here is cheery to the point of seeming programmed."

"Except for the gang guys that tried to rape me that first night."

"Rape you? They said they were offering you a ride."

"And you said you're a pencil-pusher for Homeland Security."

"I—"

"Only you happen to know a lot about explosives and computers and rescuing people from Lucite jail cells."

"I also know a lot about cooking and cleaning. But anyway, those gang guys aren't from St. Alban's."

"How do you know?"

"Their car had Georgia plates."

She studied me a moment. "Is that the sort of thing pencil-pushers notice?"

I got back on the subject of our kitchen helper. "I'm sure Tracy was just happy to get the job. This is a pretty tough economy for a small town like this."

"True," she said. "But that makes it even weirder that everyone in town is stupidly happy all the time."

I couldn't argue about that, so I focused on my tasks. Rachel did the same, and we continued working until we'd done all we could to make the kitchen spotless. Then we went upstairs and Rachel rewarded me by letting me watch her change into her bikini.

"I've got an idea," I said, raising my eyebrows.

"Don't even think about it, horn dog. And don't bother pouting, 'cause it's your own fault."

"My fault?"

"I can't help it if I used up all my energy being your scullery maid. So I'm going to go relax in the sun and bronze this body until I'm Brazilian."

"You can do that without feeling the slightest bit of

compassion for my, ah, predicament?"

"Yup. Oh, and I'll be completely unavailable sexually until…" she looked at her watch. "Three o'clock. If you can't wait that long, you'll just have to find another way to work off your frustration."

I smiled. "I know just the thing!"

"Eew."

"Eew?"

"Men. Ugh."

I had no idea what she meant, but when she headed to the beach I changed into my khaki shorts, grabbed an EpiPen, and drove back to the sand dune that housed the fire ant colony.

16.

"ARE YOU ALL set for the pig roast?" Tracy asked, cheerfully. "I've never been to a Fourth of July pig roast, never even eaten a roast pig. Have you ever even roasted a pig before, or is this your first time?"

"Tracy," Rachel said. "Shut the fuck up and let us work!"

"Sorry, I talk when I'm nervous."

"I talk when I'm nervous," Rachel said, in a high-pitched voice filled with sarcasm.

"It's okay, Trace," I said, and caught a warning look from Rachel.

It was the last Monday in June and we'd had an unexpected run on the kitchen. We'd just finished serving our first standing-room-only when a charter bus pulled up in front of the inn and dumped twenty-four female senior citizens in our doorway. Beth had taken one look at the crowd and raced out the door to make a grocery run. I was frying some maple sausage links with sliced apples to take the edge off their appetite until she returned. Rachel was squeezing oranges as fast as she could, and Tracy was washing a rack of glasses, waiting for Rachel to fill the first pitcher with orange juice.

Oh, and Rachel was getting a bit testy.

"You don't have to take up for Little Miss Tits," she informed me. "Though I don't blame you. She's done everything she can to get your attention, short of giving you a blow job."

"Oh my!" Tracy said.

"Rachel," I said. "Relax. And Tracy?"

"Yes sir?"

"No blow jobs."

She looked at me without expression.

"I mean it, okay?"

She giggled. "I wouldn't even know how."

"I wouldn't even know how!" Rachel mocked. She grabbed an orange and hurled it at Tracy's head. It missed by an inch and continued picking up speed until it slammed into the side wall of the dining room.

Tracy's lip began trembling. Her eyes filled with tears.

An elderly woman screamed in the dining room.

Which caused Tracy to scream and run out the back door. Or maybe it was the knife Rachel held, or the curl of her lip, or the gleam in her eye. I poked my head through the serving area, smiled, and said, "Where you folks from?"

One of the ladies was halfway out of her chair, but she paused when she saw me. The others appeared nervous, but hadn't bolted yet. She sat back down, tentatively. A lady sitting at her table said, "We're from Valdosta."

I glanced back at Rachel and gave her a look of disapproval. In return, she flipped her middle finger at me. I turned back to the ladies, showed them my best smile and, doing my best to imitate the friendly banter used by the locals, said, "Well, we're mighty glad to have you folks with us today, and that's a fact!"

"You sure about that?" the lady said, pointing at the dripping orange stain on the wall.

"I'm sorry, I should have warned you," I said. "It's an old St. Alban's custom. Like the ceremonial pitch in a baseball game, it's our way of welcoming you to The Seaside."

The group looked skeptical, but rewarded my bullshit with light, scattered applause. The lady doing all the talking said, "I've been to St. Alban's before, but no one ever threw an orange at me, or screamed in the kitchen."

One of the other women said, "You'd think they'd throw something softer."

Another said, "Or at least something less messy."

Another responded, "Well, it's Florida, after all."

The Valdosta lady said, "You're missing the point. They shouldn't be throwing anything at all."

I said, "Your appetizers will be out shortly."

The lady who thought we should be hurling something softer said, "Come here, Sonny Boy, I want to show you something."

I walked over to her. She pulled out her wallet and opened it to a picture of a baby.

"This is my new granddaughter," she said proudly. "Isn't she gorgeous?"

I hoped my wince wasn't obvious. Was she kidding me? Personally, I thought the little freak looked like Moms Mabley. But I smiled and said, "Wow!"

She kissed the picture and put it away. I turned and started heading back to the kitchen, thankful she didn't feel obliged to show me the rest of her brood. But after I'd gotten a few steps I saw another photo, one I recognized from the posters around town.

"Is that Libby Vail?" I said, pointing to a small photo another lady was studying.

She smiled a kindly smile and said, "I pray for her every night."

"Where'd you get it?"

"They sell them at the tourist shops on Main, near the old train depot. Such a sad story."

I nodded and continued my journey to the kitchen.

Though I didn't get a chance to tell Tracy, I was, in fact, well prepared for the Fourth of July pig roast. A full house for the B&B meant six couples, and they'd been booked months before Rachel and I showed up. We were counting on a double capacity breakfast Saturday and Sunday, and since the Fourth fell on Sunday this year, Beth had talked me into doing a giant pig roast on the beach Sunday night. We'd put a sign in the window and sold a hundred tickets at forty bucks each. After food costs and labor, Beth should net a cool three grand.

Other than losing Tracy and having to clean the orange mess from the wall, we managed to get the charter bus ladies fed without incident. Having one less set of tits in the kitchen seemed to have a calming influence on Rachel, but I knew she wasn't up to handling the entire food service alone during the busiest week of the year. She'd turn on me for sure, and probably with knives instead of oranges. Knowing the rest of the week would be difficult for Rachel, I persuaded Beth to hire two of her lady friends to start that afternoon and work through the holiday weekend. I even managed to get Tracy back, though it required an apology from Rachel.

"I'm sorry I threw an orange at you," Rachel said.

"That's okay," Tracy said.

"And?" I said.

"And I'm sorry your big fat titties flop out whenever Kevin's around," Rachel said.

"That's okay," Tracy said.

It wasn't much of an apology, but Tracy needed the job.

17.

LIKE SKINNING A cat, there are many ways to roast a pig. The most common is on a rotisserie over a fire pit. But since the right type of rotisserie costs hundreds of dollars and would have taken too long to ship, I defaulted to the ancient Mumu method of burying the pig and cooking it with hot rocks.

The art of cooking an entire animal underground was perfected by thieves in the mountains of Crete, who used to dig pits, build fires in them, and bake large stones until they became white-hot. Then they'd steal some lambs or goats, throw them in the pit, and cover them with leaves and dirt. These pits were so well insulated that the thieves could stand on top of them comfortably in bare feet during the cooking phase, even as the animal's owners came looking for them. This manner of cooking produced no smoke or odor, so the stolen animals seemed to have disappeared into thin air. Ten or twelve hours later, after the owners had given up looking for their stock, the thieves would dig up the perfectly cooked meat and enjoy the feast. Then they'd bury the remains in the pit, a perfect crime.

I roped off an area behind The Seaside and spent a couple of hours on Saturday digging the pit. Then I filled it with Georgia fat wood and local kindling. Around two o'clock, Hardware Store Earl and two of his sons picked me up in the family truck to steal some cooking rocks off the shore of

Fernandina Beach, near Fort Clinch State Park. To be precise, these were ballast stones from 1800s shipping fleets that had been tossed overboard by crew members in order to make their ships light enough to anchor close to shore. After a few hours of wading, lifting and carrying, we'd gathered enough stones to fill the pit. As we started loading the stones into the truck, the strangest thing happened. The wind that had been blowing from the south shifted slightly to the east, and a chill hit the air for a split second. I looked out to sea and saw a storm gathering on the horizon.

We loaded a few more stones as the wind started whipping the shore, lifting sand crystals into the air and hurling them at everything in its path, including the four of us. I shielded my eyes and chanced looking out to sea. While the sun behind us shone brightly, the sky before us was jet black, above a dark ocean of angry whitecaps and menacing waves.

It was that uneasy moment when one force of nature is about to take on another.

A long, low, distant rumble served as our warning, and another chilling gust of wind hit us from the east. The saw grass around us began bending at a severe angle. Somewhere behind us, a screen door slammed against its casing, threatening to burst its hinges. I'd never seen such a powerful storm appear out of nowhere, but here she was, picking up speed, heading our way.

"Better jump in the truck!" Earl said, so we did, and just as we closed the doors all hell broke loose, and the wind made the most godawful shrieking and howling noise I'd ever heard. It sounded almost like a child's shrill wail, and I could have sworn I heard cursing in at least three of the four languages I speak. It was so loud we covered our ears with our hands and winced in pain. The sky was dark around us, and the rain pelted our car so hard I could barely see ten feet out the window. I thought of the fragile screen door and looked to see if it had taken flight.

I couldn't see the ground floor of the store, because the rain was hitting the street and bouncing up several feet, making the visibility twice as poor. But something on the roof caught my eye, a shape so incongruous and absurd I hesitate to even mention it. Just to clarify, I've never seen anything like it before or since, and I'm not even sure I saw it then. As I said, the storm was all-consuming, and visibility practically nil.

It appeared to be a young woman.

If I had to guess, the shape I saw could have been a teenage girl, with long black hair and eyes that seemed to glow yellow, with a vertical black line in the center, like a jungle cat.

Fine, I know what you're thinking, but guess what: it gets even crazier!

She was laughing.

Right, I know. But if it was a young woman standing on the roof with her arms raised heavenward, she seemed to be looking right at me, and yes, she was laughing. Laughing or howling or wailing…and if I hadn't known better I could have sworn the shrieking sound that I'd believed to be the wind, was actually coming from her! Okay, I've told you what I saw, and now you can haul me away, because when I blinked my eyes and craned my neck, trying to get a better look at her, she disappeared.

Yeah, that's right. She disappeared into thin air.

I was about to ask the others if they'd seen her, but…

But the hail started.

My previous encounters with hail had been small pebbles that grew to larger pebbles, and then back to small as the storms came to an end. These hail storms were loud and fun and sometimes damaged a car's paint job. Earl's truck was several tones of rust, primer, and in a few places, actual paint, so paint damage wouldn't have been an issue in any case.

But the St. Alban's hail didn't work that way. It started huge, the size of cranberries, and quickly escalated to golf balls that hit us so hard and loud it actually drowned out the sound of the shrieking. Or maybe the shrieking had stopped when the hail showed up.

Either way, the pounding was non-stop. Unyielding. The damage to Earl's truck quickly moved beyond a simple paint job, as the windshield cracked in several places and jagged lines were spidering in all directions across the glass. The rear window was faring even worse, with numerous impact points that looked like bullet holes.

Nor was the damage confined to the windows, as hail relentlessly hammered dents into the hood of the truck. From the sound above us, I knew the roof would be even worse. The sound of hail on metal was so intense, it sounded like Blue Man Group was pounding the truck with sledgehammers during a prolonged finale.

"Holy shit!" one of the boys yelled, and the rest of us laughed.

"How you like them apples, city boy?" Earl shouted, though the hail hadn't got quite to apple size, to my knowledge.

"It's amazing the windows are still intact!" I shouted.

"They won't last much longer," Earl yelled.

Then, as suddenly as it started, it was over.

Except for one delayed crash, where something fell from the sky and struck the truck bed so hard it shook the chassis and buckled the tires.

"The fuck was that?" Earl shouted.

The sudden silence was so strange, we all just sat there a moment. We looked out the windows, then at each other. We'd come through it, whatever it was, and the four of us had a story to tell for the rest of our days.

"Don't get out yet," Earl said. "Whatever that last one was, might not be the last one of 'em."

I agreed. "That wasn't a hailstone," I said.

"What then?"

I thought a minute. "Could be a meteorite, or a piece of a space satellite falling to earth."

"In the middle of a hailstorm?"

"Best guess. Of course, we could always just get out of the truck and take a look."

"You first, then," Earl said.

We started laughing. The sun came back out and I climbed out of the truck and the others followed. Then we looked in the back and found what had made the noise.

Not a meteorite.

Not a piece of a space satellite.

It was a cannonball.

"Someone fired a cannonball at us?" I said.

"Never know," one of Earl's kids said. "This used to be a pirate town. Lotta people still think of themselves as pirates."

"Probably just got picked up by the storm, carried awhile, and dropped on the back of my truck when the wind died down," Earl said.

"Looks ancient," I said.

Earl took the ball from me and inspected it carefully. He removed his cap and scratched his head. "Now this here might be worth something," he said. He placed it on the floor of his truck.

We finished loading the ballast rocks into the back of the

truck and talked about the storm, comparing it to everything else we'd experienced in nature.

At four the next morning I built a huge fire in the pit and roasted the stones for more than two hours. Then Earl and his sons helped me wrap most of the pig in aluminum foil and carry it out to the pit. We removed a few of the small center stones and stuffed them inside the pig to facilitate the cooking. The hot stones created a lot of smoke and loud sizzling sounds as the pig seared from within. We wrapped the rest of the pig in foil and placed it carefully in the pit, and covered it with banana leaves and hot stones. Then I removed the ropes I'd used to cordon off the area, and raked a couple of feet of sand over the top of the pit. By the time we finished, if you didn't know where the pig was cooking, it would be impossible to tell.

Satisfied with our effort, Earl, the boys and me went back inside and I fed them some shrimp grits and country ham biscuits with redeye gravy. We sat and talked about the storm and drank coffee.

At one point I asked them if they'd seen anything on the roof of the store.

"Like what?" Earl said.

"I don't know, I just thought I saw something up there."

"Like a cannon?" one of the sons said.

We all laughed and I changed the subject.

Beth came down to start putting things in order for the big Fourth of July breakfast, and I got up to help her. The men left. It felt comfortable, the two of us working together. We didn't talk much, and didn't feel like we needed to.

The way I figured, it would take about eleven hours for the pig to be fall-off-the-bone perfect, which meant dinner would be ready around six o'clock. In the meantime our guests could enjoy the beach, play golf, or shop in nearby Fernandina Beach. Rachel and Tracy would serve drinks to the beach group, Beth would run a shuttle service for the others, and I'd handle an all-day food and beverage shift. The pig roast would be over by eight-thirty, at which time we'd shuttle our dozen house guests to the big fireworks display at the Fernandina Beach marina. All in all, it would be a Fourth of July to remember.

At least that's what I planned.

Unfortunately, none of those things happened.

Except for the memorable part.

18.

IT HAD BEEN a rough couple of weeks for D'Augie.

First, he'd nearly died on a sand dune swarming with fire ants. Then he'd been saved by Donovan Creed, the man he tried to kill, a situation made no less mortifying to D'Augie after hearing that Creed and his girlfriend stripped him naked during the rescue. And of course Creed had stolen his prized knife, the only gift D'Augie had ever gotten from his father.

Then Rachel told him that Creed took a caretaker's job at The Seaside Bed & Breakfast, where he planned to rid the attic of squirrel infestation. So D'Augie snuck out of the hospital and hid in The Seaside's attic, hoping to catch Creed by surprise. But the surprise turned out to be on D'Augie, who broke an arm and leg after being attacked by angry attic snakes and hungry squirrels.

After dragging his broken body a quarter-mile to his car, it took a superhuman effort to make the forty-minute drive to Jackson Memorial, where ER personnel set his fractures and re-treated his festering fire ant bites.

During the course of his treatment, D'Augie had an allergic reaction to one of the antibiotics they administered, and nearly died again. He spent more than a week mildly sedated as they pumped him with steroids and painkillers. Eventually they got him back to normal, if you can call an arm and leg cast normal. Worse, both casts were on the right side, which made it impossible for D'Augie to drive a car.

But D'Augie was nothing if not determined, and he aimed to kill Creed. He'd traveled more than a thousand miles over two years to get the man who killed his father, and he wasn't going to give up because of some plaster.

He hired a cab to pick him up at the hospital and take him to one of the airport motels. He'd wanted to stay at the Amelia Island Resort, or in Fernandina Beach, but it was Saturday, July third, and everything on the island was booked. He got a second cab to take him to Wal-Mart, where he bought a buck knife, a sharpening tool, some food, and several bottles of water. He spent most of the night putting a fine edge on his blade. Next morning he put his supplies in his shoulder bag, caught a cab to St. Alban's and told the driver to let him out two blocks south of The Seaside Bed & Breakfast. The driver did so and D'Augie gave him a fifty and said he'd catch a ride back with a friend.

D'Augie's arm cast was more of an inconvenience than a problem. It could actually be considered a benefit, since the sling that held it in place could be used to conceal his knife. But moving around with the leg cast was proving to be an issue. The cast ran from his ankle to the top of his thigh, and forced him to turn sideways every time he took a step with his right foot.

His right foot was bare, since the nature of the cast's construction prevented him from wearing a shoe. He supposed he could wear a giant sock, but he didn't happen to own any giant socks and hadn't thought to buy one.

Now, standing on the street, watching the cab drive away, D'Augie wished he'd thought to buy a dozen socks. The thought came to him when he realized he was standing on a live cigarette. D'Augie cried out and lifted his bare foot off the pavement, hoping to get relief. But his leg cast caused him to pitch forward. In order to keep from falling face first, he had to plant his casted foot back on the street. Even though the smoldering cigarette was inches behind him at this point, the noon sun had rendered the pavement blazingly hot, a situation that worsened the wound he'd received from the cigarette. He yelled again, lifted his leg again, spun sideways and was again forced to put his casted foot back on the hot pavement to keep his balance. Unfortunately, that step burned the tender bottom of his foot even worse, and he screeched. He lifted his foot again, spun sideways again, nearly fell again, put it down again, screamed again, and kept repeating the process, over and over, like some "cast" member from *Night of the Living Dead*.

D'Augie did manage to accomplish something he hadn't meant to do. It was imperative, his doctor had said, that D'Augie not attempt to walk forward without first turning his leg to one side. Otherwise, the top of his cast would cut into his left thigh and chafe it badly.

The doctor had been right about the pain. D'Augie could feel the cast tearing into the flesh of his upper left thigh. Up to now, though he'd traveled a distance of maybe five feet in forty seconds, he'd been yelping every time he took a step with the right foot. Now he was also crying out with every step of his left. He knew he must look like some kind of freak show, hopping and spinning and screaming and tearing his flesh as he kept circling round and round.

Eventually, he got dizzy and fell face-first into the pavement. The good news was, his arm absorbed most of the blow and his right foot finally stopped hurting. The bad news was, the arm that broke his fall was the same one he'd recently broken. In addition, he sustained a cut forehead and what felt like a severely broken nose.

"Motherfucker!" he screamed to the sky.

The young man making love to the older woman in the rental unit twenty yards away heard the scream as if it were just outside the window. Rattled, he jumped up and ran to the window, looked around the yard, but saw nothing.

"What's wrong?" his friend's mother said.

"Someone's watching us."

"That's ridiculous."

"Seriously. Some guy just called me a motherfucker, and since you're a mother…"

"The weed's made you paranoid," she said. "Come back to bed."

He lay bleeding in the street. He wanted to cry, but he was too angry. He screamed the word again, louder this time: "Motherfucker!" — and thought he heard a young man shout "Jason? Is that you?"

He cocked his head, listening, but didn't hear it again. D'Augie lay in the street, trying to imagine what could possibly be worse, and then came up with this: How about if a truck was barreling down the highway, directly in his path, refusing to slow down?

Because that's exactly what was happening.

D'Augie rolled onto his side and screamed, then onto his back and screamed, then onto his other side and screamed, then his front and screamed, and repeated the cycle until he'd gotten out of the truck's path—just in time. He raised his good arm and flipped his middle finger and cursed. The reason for his rolling screams were twofold: first, he hadn't realized it at the time, but the recent fall on the pavement had rebroken his arm. Worse, he'd stabbed himself in the chest several times with the knife he'd hidden in his sling.

96

The one he'd spent all night sharpening.

Inside the rental unit the young man was freaking out.

"You didn't hear that? It sounded like your son screaming at me."

"Jason's in Jacksonville with his father. Look, you're so wound up; I'm going to do something special to help you relax. Now just lie down and close your eyes..."

Outside the window D'Augie lay on the side of the street and bled a few minutes and tried to formulate a plan of attack. He eventually came to the conclusion that his best bet was to walk into the front entrance of The Seaside and locate Creed. The sand would be hot on his bare foot, but not as hot as the pavement. He should be able to handle it. Once inside the B&B, he'd ask Creed for help stopping the bleeding, and stab him first chance he got. He'd send Creed straight to hell.

As soon as he got to his feet.

Which he suddenly found impossible to do.

"Cocksucker!" he roared at the sky. "You goddamned cocksucker!"

The older woman heard the word both times. She lifted her head and looked at her lover's face. His eyes were closed and he was grinning from ear to ear.

"You little bastard!" she shouted. "You think that's funny? You and your little friend hiding in the bushes, making fun of me? Get out of here! Now!" She ran to the window. "Hey, asshole in the bushes: get the fuck off my property or I'll call the cops!"

D'Augie removed the knife from his sling and held it in his left hand, then began rolling through the sand and sea oats toward the B&B, wondering how there could be ten thousand people between here and Fernandina Beach today, but not a soul within sight to help him to his feet. Worse, some lady had just screamed at him and threatened to call the cops! D'Augie was astounded by the lack of compassion in St. Alban's. He heard a young man shout, "What did I do?"

"Get out!" the lady screamed again.

She didn't sound friendly, but D'Augie could hardly afford to be picky. He needed assistance.

"Help me!" he shouted.

"Help you? Sure, I'll help you! I'm getting my shotgun. If you're still laying in the bushes when I get back, I'm going to blow your ass to hell!

D'Augie cursed, and started rolling. It was slow, hot, exhausting work trying to roll two blocks to the inn. Sand had caked on the cuts in his forehead and entered his broken nose. He held his breath and tried to blow the blockage from his nostrils. In doing so, he remembered watching a fight on TV once, where the corner man told his fighter never to blow a broken nose.

But why? D'Augie tried to remember. Oh yeah: because it will swell up and hurt ten times worse.

The corner man had been right.

D'Augie kept rolling. He figured to make it to the gate and use the gate pole to prop himself up. But the gate was a block and a half away, and D'Augie was in serious pain, losing blood, and getting dizzy. His mind was getting fuzzy, and he was stuck amid the sand dunes. He stopped rolling for a minute and took a break, trying to remember what it was about laying on a sand dune that posed a problem.

The fire ants brought his memory back. Ten or twelve of them had gotten in his shirt and began stinging the back of his neck. D'Augie wasn't about to let them grow in numbers like the last time. He resumed his rolling, and though the dune sand was soft and loose and the going much slower, he made up for it by working harder.

Ten minutes later he found himself not in front of the B&B as he'd planned, but behind and to the side of it. He broke out of the last sand dune and rolled onto the compacted sand behind the inn. He was lying about thirty feet from the boardwalk, near its center. From his vantage point he figured it was a hundred and fifty feet from the beach to the inn, and he could see the steps at both ends. Eight steps on the left end took you up to the inn, and however many steps there were on the right end would take you down to the beach. The boardwalk was elevated about two feet above the sand, and there were access points on either side, with three steps each. There were people below him on the beach. He couldn't see them and couldn't be seen by them, but he could hear them laughing and playing. He also heard Rachel calling to Creed, hollering for four more Kashenkas, which D'Augie knew to be some sort of drink. He turned his head and saw her standing on the boardwalk, maybe twenty feet to his left. She had her hands cupped around her mouth and was concentrating her attention on the back of the inn, and hadn't noticed him lying in the sand.

D'Augie thought about calling out to her, maybe get her to lift him up and help him to the kitchen, but when he heard Creed shout back that he'd bring the drinks to her in a minute, he came up with a better plan, one he'd seen in the movie *Jeremiah Johnson*, starring Robert Redford. In the movie, an Indian had buried himself under a layer of snow and jumped out and attacked Robert Redford. It didn't work, but then again, Redford had been holding a rifle, whereas Creed would be carrying a tray of exotic drinks. D'Augie would simply roll a few feet closer, over to that loose, fresh-raked sand by the boardwalk, bury himself a foot or two into it, and when

Creed passed by, he'd jump up and use the edge of the boardwalk to get to his feet. Then he'd come up behind Creed from under the boardwalk and cut the tendon in Creed's ankle. Creed's scream would be drowned out by the beach noises, and when he fell, D'Augie would slit his throat and make his getaway.

D'Augie remained perfectly still until Rachel disappeared down the steps to the beach. Then he rolled to the fresh-raked area and positioned the knife in his cast. He began digging the soft sand out from under his body with his left hand. It was easier than he'd expected. Within minutes he scooped out an area about a foot deep and eased his back into it, and started covering himself with the sand he'd dug out of the hole.

After a few minutes of that, he realized it wasn't going to work. With only one free hand and leg he wasn't going to be able to cover himself enough to escape detection.

D'Augie would just have to roll out of the hole, make his way to the boardwalk, lift himself up, and intercept Creed from the front. Creed would probably be taken back encountering the limping, bleeding sand-covered D'Augie, but the last thing he'd expect is to be attacked. So the element of surprise, plus the fact that Creed would be carrying a tray of drinks, would be enough to tip the scales of battle in D'Augie's favor. So that's what he'd do.

As soon as he worked his way out of the hole he'd dug.

Which he suddenly didn't seem capable of doing.

And worse, his back was getting awfully goddamned hot for some reason.

19.

I WAS ALONE in the kitchen when I heard Rachel shouting a drink order from the boardwalk. I'd served a few of our guests Kashenkas earlier, and knew they'd be ordering them all afternoon.

The Kashenka is a trendy drink invented in Paris twenty years ago to honor a beautiful Polish cabaret dancer who worked near the Ritz hotel. It's made with pressed strawberries, white castor sugar and Polish vodka and served in a tall glass filled with cracked ice.

I figured if Rachel was calling for drinks instead of sending Tracy to the kitchen for them, both girls were obviously needed on the beach to tend to our demanding guests. My immediate problem was the lack of serving trays. I looked under the sink, in the hutch and even tried the broom closet, but couldn't find anything suitable for presenting the drinks. Maybe the guests wouldn't mind if I just used a dinner plate. I had just started trimming the strawberries, when I remembered the picnic basket Beth had taken to her sick friend.

The basket was on the counter, filled with apples. I took the apples out and turned the basket upside down to make sure it was clean, and noticed some scratch marks on the bottom. There was something unusual about them. They seemed to be less random and more of a deliberate design. I took the basket close to the back door to get as much light on it as possible, and realized what I was seeing was not scratches at all, but two distinct Roman numerals. I rubbed my thumb over the woven wood where the scratches had been made, and felt something sharp. I pried apart the area between the weave and discovered something had been wedged in there.

It was that exact moment I heard a man screaming. I cocked my head to the side to listen. It sounded like a Rebel yell, only louder, and more terrifying.

I dropped the basket, tore out the door and raced about twenty feet down the boardwalk and found a man lying in the pig pit. I hopped over the rail and got to him quickly and pulled him out and turned him over. He had a leg and arm cast and his shirt had scorch marks on the back. A few more minutes and this guy would have been burned alive. I turned him on his side and felt his pulse for ten seconds.

Though he was in serious pain, I could see he was going to live. He'd probably have permanent burn marks on his back, and might require skin grafts. His face and hair were caked with blood and sand and something about him seemed familiar. His eyes were wild with pain, and he was grabbing at his sling. I looked around for help and saw that no one seemed to have heard him or noticed me pull him from the pit.

"Don't move," I said. "I'll be right back."

I ran back to the kitchen, grabbed my cell phone and dialed 911 and gave them the details. I grabbed four bottles of water from the refrigerator and a roll of paper towels and ran back to the burn victim, who was trying to roll toward the sand dunes. I stopped him and turned him on his stomach and began pouring water over his back. I decided not to remove his shirt in case the skin might come off with it. I poured a second bottle of water on his back and then turned him on his side and opened a third bottle and poured it on his face and hair. I got him to drink a few swallows from my last bottle of water, and used the remainder to wet some paper towels. I dabbed at his face with the moistened towels, and though his broken nose threw me off a minute, I finally recognized him as the kid Rachel and I had pulled off the sand dune a couple of weeks earlier.

Only this time he had a broken arm and a full leg cast. And he was digging at his arm cast again, and shouting incoherently. Whatever he'd been trying to do to his broken arm, he stopped doing, and grabbed my throat instead.

I could tell the kid was trying to strangle me, but he was so weak he couldn't have crushed a grape. He seemed happy doing it though, so I let him keep trying. While he did, my thoughts turned to damage control. If he decided to sue Beth, she'd lose everything. But would he sue her? Of course he would—it's the American way.

Maybe I could buy him off, I thought. Whatever he hoped to gain from suing Beth would be a pittance to me. So we'd be okay from that angle. I'd take care of his doctor bills and give him double whatever he wanted from Beth.

With that concern out of the way, I wondered about the pig roast. I had a hundred paid guests coming for pork in a few hours. Could I salvage the dinner? I looked around and saw a few people here and there, but no one seemed to be paying attention to us, so sure, I could cover the pit up again and no one would need to know about the kid burning in it.

Unless he told someone.

I looked down at him and wondered if I should just kill him. I mean, I'd probably be doing him a favor, since this had to be the most accident-prone kid who ever lived. He'd die on his own if I'd just stop saving him.

But no, it wouldn't be right to kill someone just to keep from canceling a pig roast. And anyway the kid couldn't have known there was a pig roasting under his back. Maybe he'd figure it out later, and I could buy his silence before he blabbed it. In that event, maybe I could salvage dinner after all.

Except that the EMS guys would be on the scene within moments, and they'd have questions about the burn marks on his back. Could I set a quick fire and pretend he'd fallen into it? No. A good cover-up requires planning.

I'd just have to cancel the pig roast.

With that decision behind me, I started wondering a few things about the kid. Like why was he trying to strangle me? And why was he here? How did he break his nose and arm and leg? What had he been doing on the fire ant hill with the buck knife?

I thought about the knife a minute, and how it had fallen out of his pants pocket when the EMS came the last time. I reached into his sling and found a similar knife under his broken arm.

I was beginning to think this kid was trying to kill me.

I thought about his broken bones and wondered if they could have been sustained by falling through the plywood attic access door.

Killing this kid might be a good idea after all, I thought.

But then I heard the sirens from the EMS truck heading our way. I ran to the kitchen, hid the knife, and went out the front door to flag them down.

20.

THE EMS CREW alerted the Health Department about the roast pig pit to make sure we didn't serve our guests pork that could be tainted—a ridiculous assertion that made me wonder how we ever became such a pansy-ass country. I mean, a guy burns his back on heated sand almost twelve inches above the rocks that are cooking a pig. The guy never touched the pig, so what's the big deal?

The Health Department contacted the Humane Society, but since they were busy manning a float in the Fernandina Beach Fourth of July parade we had to wait until after the ribbons had been awarded. They came in third, in case you care.

Eventually they came and confiscated the pig, which meant that I had everything I needed for the pig roast except the pig. After the EMS crew rushed the kid to the hospital I made a run to the closest Winn-Dixie and bought four large, spiral-cut hams and several pounds of bacon. I couldn't call it a pig roast, but I could fry up the ham in bacon grease and give our customers a meal they'd never forget.

"How many did we end up with after you offered the full refund?" Beth asked.

We were in the kitchen. It was a half-hour till midnight on a long, hot day, and I was exhausted. We all were. "Amazingly, we salvaged them all," I said.

"Knocking ten dollars off the price helped," Rachel added.

Beth nodded. "Thanks, guys. You were both great today." She looked at me. "Any word on that kid they took to the hospital?"

Rachel surprised me by saying, "His name is D'Augie."

"Doggie?"

"Yeah. But it's not spelled that way. Anyway, I talked to the doctor. He's going to be okay. He doesn't need grafts or anything."

"You ever figure out what he was doing in your fire pit?" Beth asked.

"Not a clue," I said.

Beth covered her mouth and tried to suppress a yawn, gave up, and let it run its course without apology. "Okay, I'm done," she said. "Love you, guys."

We said our goodnights and waited a few minutes for Beth to settle into her bedroom and close her bathroom door. When we heard the water running in Beth's sink I handed Rachel the picnic basket and told her to turn it over.

"You see anything unusual?" I said.

She passed it back to me. "I'm really tired, Kevin."

She started for the staircase.

"Rachel," I said. "It's important."

She paused and frowned. "Can we do this tomorrow?"

"Ten seconds. I swear."

"This has been the longest day ever. I hate waiting on people. I'm tired. I want to go to bed."

I put my finger to my lips, signaling her to quiet her voice. I whispered, "You wanted to know what's going on with Beth, right? Why she's acting so weird?"

Her eyes lit up, and she walked over to me. "She's got a guy? And what, they went on a picnic?" Rachel cocked her head, putting the pieces together. Her face broke into a wide grin. "Oh my God! Little Miss Stick-up-her-ass is getting banged by some local yokel outdoors and passing him off as a sick friend! Who is it, someone we know?"

I was amazed how her mind worked. I motioned her to follow me back to the kitchen. I gave her the picnic basket and pointed to what I'd originally thought were random scratch marks.

"Look at these scratches closely," I said, "and tell me what you see."

Rachel gave me a skeptical look, but she squinted to bring the marks into focus. "It's just a bunch of—wait, it looks like Roman numerals. Fifty-five, right?"

"So it would appear."

"Beth's boyfriend is fifty-five?"

I smiled. "Maybe she banged him fifty-five times and wanted to mark the milestone."

"That's ridiculous!"

"I agree."

Rachel frowned. "You're an asshole."

I arched my brows.

She continued. "You're standing here, letting me go on and on, but telling me nothing. You know I'm tired and you're deliberately wasting my time."

I nodded. "Let me get right to it. I don't think the L and V are Roman numerals."

"You don't."

"Nuh uh."

"But for some reason I'm supposed to give a shit why."

"They're initials."

She thought about that a moment, then said, "Beth's boyfriend?"

"If it is, it should be easy to find him," I said. "Not too many people around here with a last name that starts with a V."

She eyed me carefully. "But you don't think it's her boyfriend."

"Nope."

"Because?"

"These initials were scratched by a woman."

"Uh, don't freak when I tell you, but Beth's a woman." She saw me grinning and added, "Wait. How do you know these marks were made by a woman?"

"They were made by a fingernail."

"And what, men don't have fingernails?"

"Let me continue. This is Beth's picnic basket. If she were labeling it, she'd have used an ink pen, or a knife or other sharp object."

"And she'd have used her own initials."

"Exactly."

"So maybe she's got a fuck buddy with the initials LV. They go on a picnic, spread out a big blanket, eat some food, and suddenly he's all over her. She's all 'Oh, LV! LV!' They have wild monkey sex right in the middle of the day in some deserted area tucked behind a sand dune. It's their special place. They're lying on the blanket after doing it, thoroughly spent, and our sanctimonious little Beth is all raptured up 'cause it's been a long time, and she gathers up her strength and scratches his initials on the basket."

I looked at her as I often did, with complete amazement. "Why is it that all your scenarios involve sex?"

"Why is it that yours don't?"

She had me there. I decided to move along. "Let's frame it a different way."

She shrugged.

"You still haven't proven the marks were made by a woman."

"I'm getting to that."

"You're just trying to be dramatic. Like some detective in a stupid movie."

"It's my one opportunity."

"When you fall asleep tonight I might superglue your dick to your stomach."

I looked at her as I often did, with complete horror. I handed her the little sharp piece I'd put in my pocket earlier, just before the kid burned his back in my fire pit. She looked at it and wrinkled her nose, turned her hand and let it fall to the kitchen counter.

"That's disgusting," she said.

"But you'll concede it's a woman's fingernail?"

"Not Beth's."

"Right, not Beth's. But a woman's. And suppose she was scratching her own initials into the bottom of the basket, and had to use her fingernail because she didn't have access to an ink pen, a knife, or any other type of sharp object."

"Like what, a prisoner?"

"Exactly like a prisoner, except that she has a northern accent."

"A northern accent."

"Yup."

"And this you can tell from her fingernail."

I smiled, enjoying the moment.

Rachel abruptly crossed the floor to the cabinet that housed the odds and ends. She pushed a few objects around with her finger and eventually picked up a small tube and held it between her thumb and forefinger so I could see it clearly.

Super Glue.

She sighed. "I'm tired, Kevin. Just say it. Who do you think made these scratches in Beth's picnic basket?"

"Libby Vail."

21.

A LONG, LOW rumble woke us up an hour before dawn. Remembering what happened the last time I heard that sound, I jumped out of bed and checked the window, wondering if another hailstorm was headed our way. Thankfully, all was calm. Patches of heat lightning lit up the distant sky.

"You okay?" I said.

Rachel murmured, "I'm tired. Go back to sleep."

"How'd you know the kid's name?"

"What kid?" She seemed half asleep as she said it.

I raised the volume in my voice to a conversational level. "The kid that got burned in the pig pit yesterday, the fire ant kid."

She lay still a moment, and then yawned. "I went to check on him in the hospital."

"When?"

"The morning after that thing with the fire ants."

She settled back into her breathing rhythm and I thought about that morning and how I'd gone for a long run. I remembered returning to the inn, and Beth mentioning Rachel had gone somewhere in the car. So that made sense. But Rachel had gone to see the kid *before* I agreed to help Beth at The Seaside. Which meant there was more to the story.

"You saw him again, though."

She hesitated a moment, then sighed and propped herself

up on one elbow.

"Is this really so important we have to talk about it now?"

"That depends on your answer to my last question."

She thought a minute. "Did I see him again? Yes. Why, you think I'm cheating on you?"

"No," I said, but her comment made me pause to think about the possibility. Rachel was a sexual being, and while I didn't doubt for a minute that she was capable of cheating, I didn't think the kid was physically capable of participating. Then again, he seemed awfully resilient.

Rachel said, "Then what, you think he's holding that girl captive somewhere?"

"No, I think that's a whole different thing."

"Then what's all this about D'Augie?"

"When you saw him that second time, did you happen to mention I'd taken the job as caretaker and that I was planning to kill the squirrels in the attic?"

She started to speak, but caught herself. She thought about it. "You think he somehow got up in the attic that day when all the snakes and squirrels got out?"

"There was a major hole in the plywood, where the stairs are," I said. "Him falling through it might explain the casts on his arm and leg."

"Why on earth would he want to climb up into that smelly old attic?"

"To kill me."

She laughed. "*Kill* you? He doesn't even *know* you! Kill you for what?"

I kissed her forehead. "That's the million-dollar question, isn't it?"

She looked at me wide-eyed. "Are you for real? D'Augie's sweet. I think he's just a weird, accident-prone kid."

"Remember the knife I found that first night?"

"Yeah. You didn't tell me about it at first, though, remember? I found it in the dresser."

"Well, he had another one yesterday, in his arm sling."

"So?"

"This knife was just as sharp as the first one."

She shook her head. "Kevin, you're insane."

"Why's that?"

"Every time we see this kid he's lying helpless on his back in the sand. One day he's getting bit half to death by fire ants, the next he's getting burned alive in a pig pit. Not to mention the fact he's hopping around on a broken leg and has a broken arm. You really think he's trying to kill you?"

"I didn't say he was any good at it."

"Go to sleep."

I took a seat on the couch and waited until Rachel had fallen into a deep sleep, which didn't take long, thanks to the sleeping pill I'd given her a few hours earlier. I put on my running shoes and shorts and snuck out of the room and jogged the mile to the little church on Eighth Street. I paused, waiting for the feeling, but nothing was happening. I circled the building, peering through windows, searching for any sign of guards or prisoners, but found nothing.

Maybe the feel-good power hadn't come from the church after all. On the chance it was further north, I jogged another quarter-mile up A1A, gave up, circled back around to Eighth Street, and stopped about two blocks west of the church.

Still no feeling.

Assuming the power could be detected at least a mile from its source, I decided to cover as wide an area as possible on my way back to the B&B. The course I chose took me near the hospital on Center Street.

Which is where I finally felt it.

I didn't understand how the feeling could be at the church one day, at the hospital the next, but I knew for certain it was emanating from the hospital this time. Wishing I had a car so I could get there quicker, I tore down the street in a full sprint. As I rounded the last corner, I knew I was too late.

The feeling was getting progressively weaker.

I stopped.

Within a minute it was gone.

I jogged back to the B&B more confused than ever. When I got in the room I fired up my laptop and typed a name into the search engine while Rachel slept. In a half-hour the alarm would ring to get us up for kitchen duty. I clicked on one of the search choices and began reading. That article led me to another, and I read a half-dozen more before the alarm went off. When it did I turned the computer off and shut the lid.

Rachel pushed the button on the alarm and felt the empty bed where I was supposed to be. She sat up and looked at the bathroom, then around the room until she saw me.

"You still worried about D'Augie?"

"I still think he's trying to kill me, but that's not why I stayed up. I was thinking about Libby Vail, and how she wanted to come here to learn about her heritage."

"You really think she's alive and being held captive here?"

"I think it's possible."

"Okay, whatever. So you were wondering what, exactly?"

"There are probably a hundred cities and towns along the coast of North and South Carolina, Georgia, and Florida, right?"

"I guess."

"But Libby wanted to come to St. Alban's to research her connection to Jack Hawley, the pirate."

"So?"

"So why St. Alban's? Why not Fernandina Beach, or St. Augustine, or any of the hundred other cities and towns?"

Rachel thought about it a minute and then frowned. "Kevin, you are so full of shit. I bet you've been looking at porn this whole time."

I laughed. "Not porn, but I did find something extremely interesting."

"Uh huh," she said, unconvinced.

"I found a fascinating story about pirates in St. Alban's, and how a girl named Abby Winter may have saved the town. The story was attributed to Jack Hawley."

"Attributed," Rachel said.

"You want to hear it?"

"No. I want to pee."

She climbed out of bed and trudged to the bathroom. I turned my thoughts away from pirates and concentrated on the day ahead. The kid Rachel called D'Augie may have sucked at it, but he was definitely trying to kill me, and I intended to find out why. But since he was in the hospital in terrible shape, I decided to put him fourth on my to-do list. First on my list was making breakfast for the departing guests. Second was interviewing the most influential person in town I could find, because if Libby Vail was being held captive, the cover-up had to involve a number of people, including those at the highest level. Third was rescuing Libby Vail, assuming she was being held prisoner. Then I'd deal with this D'Augie kid who was trying to kill me.

22.

I WAS IN no rush to rescue Libby Vail. For one thing, I wasn't positive where she was. The church was still my best guess, but if she was being held there I'd have to alter my theory that she was connected in some way to the power I'd experienced.

I knew it was a huge stretch to assume she was locked in a church on a relatively busy corner in St. Alban's. My reason for having made the connection was flimsy, at best: I'd seen a lady with a picnic basket walking up the church stairs a week before Beth left The Seaside carrying a similar basket. When Beth came back I found a woman's fingernail and scratch marks on the bottom of the basket that might be L and V.

So it was a hunch, more than anything.

Against that hunch, I had to imagine church leaders going along with the kidnapping of a young coed from Pennsylvania and allowing her to be held captive in their tiny building. Since church services are held there, you'd have to wonder how Libby Vail could be rendered quiet enough that none of the church members had ever heard her crying for help. Either that or you'd have to believe the entire congregation was involved. I also had to add the FBI into the equation, since they had set up camp in St. Alban's after the kidnapping, made a thorough investigation, and came away with nothing.

If I was right about Libby Vail being held captive at the little church all this time, it would require a conspiracy that started at the very top of local government, including the mayor and chief of police.

Which is why, at 1:00 pm sharp, I had Rachel drop me off at the court house. I walked up the three stone steps in front of the building, opened the main door, and walked about halfway down the hall until I found the mayor's office. The door was open, so I entered and passed the empty desk normally occupied by Milly, the mayor's secretary. This, I deduced by channeling my inner Sherlock Holmes. To put it another way, Milly's nameplate was sitting atop the empty desk.

I knocked on the door to the mayor's office, and opened it.

"Mr. Creed," he said, rising to his feet.

We shook hands. He gestured to one of the chairs in front of his desk and said, "Sit down, sit down." When I did, he pointed at the length of rope draped over my right shoulder. "What's that for, you planning to hang me?" He laughed.

"You know me as a cook, but I'm also the maintenance man."

He looked at the rope again and frowned. I couldn't tell if he was opposed to the rope itself, or the fact I wouldn't tell him why I had it. He brightened his expression a bit and said, "That corn bread you made was the best thing I ever put in my mouth. I told my wife about it, and she said, 'Ask him what his secret ingredient is.'"

"Yogurt."

"Well hell, that can't be true. I hate yogurt."

I smiled. According to comments I'd heard from our local breakfast customers, Carl "Curly" Bradford was considered Mayor for Life by the good people of St. Alban's. He was tall and lanky, mid-forties, with sharp facial features and rust-colored hair flecked with gray. He had a stern, professorial air about him. I pointed to the bicycle hooked vertically on the far wall of his office. "You ride to work on that?"

"It's my exercise routine," he said. "I ride every day, rain or shine. Like you, except that you're a runner."

"Small town," I said.

"That, plus I've seen you running a time or two, out on A1A."

We looked at each other a minute without speaking. He seemed uncomfortable with the silence, and showed it by making small talk. "You're making quite a name for yourself as a cook."

"I won't lie, I enjoy it."

"You don't look like a cook, though."

"No?"

"Is it stressful looking after that old place?"

"Why do you ask?"

He smiled. "Couple of folks saw your car parked on A1A a few times, thought they might have seen you lying on the sand dunes."

"Is that illegal?"

"Closer to the beach it is. But not where you go, as far as I know."

I nodded.

"It's dangerous, is what it is," he said.

"How so?"

"Lot of fire ants in that area, as I guess you know. It's right near the spot where that young man nearly died from fire ant bites."

"You know anything about him?" I said.

"He's not from around here, is all I know. That, and the fact he got roasted in your fire pit."

"I heard he's going to be okay," I said.

"I heard the same thing."

"Mayor Bradford—"

"Please," he said. "If we're finally getting to it, you might as well call me Carl."

"Okay then, Carl."

He shifted in his chair. "What can I do for you, Donovan?"

"You can tell me about Libby Vail."

He didn't flinch. I know because I was watching to see if he would. Instead, he smiled and said, "Well, I don't know much more than what you're likely to have heard. Libby was a Liberal Arts major at Penn State," he said. "Her room-mate told the police that Libby had planned to come here to research her roots."

"She thought she was descended from pirates."

"Gentleman Jack Hawley," he said.

I nodded. "You folks have a monthly celebration in Libby's honor. People come from all over the world."

"They do," he said.

"It's good for business."

"As it turns out, it is. But that's not the only reason we celebrate Libby's life. We do it to keep her memory alive. The whole town has sort of adopted her."

"I guess most young people want to leave small towns like St. Alban's," I said. "But Libby wanted to come here."

"Well, I don't imagine she was planning to settle down here or anything."

"I didn't get to see the Pirate Parade yesterday," I said, "but I saw the pictures in the paper this morning."

"Sorry you missed it," he said. "It's quite an event."

"I was particularly interested in the picture of the pirate ship float," I said.

"What about it?"

"That's Hawley's ship, right?"

He rubbed his face with his right hand and yawned. "Sorry," he said. "Long weekend, too much grog."

He winked.

I nodded.

"Yeah, they've had that float forever," he said. "It's supposed to be *The Fortress*, Jack Hawley's ship. Why do you ask?"

"In the news photo, on the bridge of the boat, there's a pretty young woman standing next to the pirate."

Mayor Bradford raised an eyebrow. "She's quite a looker," he said. Then he added, "But so is your Rachel."

"I'm quite happy with Rachel," I said. "What I was wondering about is the significance of the girl on the pirate ship. From what I've read about pirates, they didn't often allow women on board their ships."

For the first time since I'd entered his office, Mayor Bradford's face registered concern. He bit the top corner of his lip. "I don't believe there's any historical significance to it," he said. "I think they're just using the float as an excuse to show off the prettiest girl in Fernandina Beach."

"Really? Because I think it might be more than that."

He cocked his head to one side and squinted at me, and as he did so, his face drew into itself and grew as stern as it could without imploding. "Why don't you just tell me what it is you're reading into that picture from the newspaper."

"I've been doing some online research on Jack Hawley, and there's a story, a legend that supposedly happened exactly three hundred years ago."

Mayor Bradford's eyes darted around the room. He looked beyond me, to the open doorway as if searching for an escape route. "A legend," he said.

"Carl," I said. "Look at me."

He did.

I said, "You've lived here all your life. You have to know what I'm talking about."

He paused a moment before speaking. "If you're referring to Abby Winter saving the town, I think that was just a story from a dime novel written back in the 1800s."

"The story I read didn't say anything about a dime novel. But it's a fascinating story either way."

"Maybe you should rewrite it."

"Maybe I will."

We sat there in silence. After a moment Carl clapped his hands and stood. "If that's it, I guess I better get going. I gave Milly the afternoon off and was about to close the office when you came in. I'm meeting the Mayor of Fernandina for a little surf casting." He pulled his bike off the bike hook and leaned it against his desk.

I stood and we shook hands again. I turned and walked to the doorway and paused.

"Was there something else?" he said.

"Yeah."

"What's that?"

"I think Libby Vail believed she was related to Jack Hawley through Abby Winter."

"That's ridiculous," he said.

"Maybe, but it would explain why she wanted to come to St. Alban's to research her lineage."

"It's been done," he blurted. Seeing my expression he realized he'd said more than he meant to. He hastily added, "What I mean is, back when Libby Vail went missing, that old story came out, the one about Abby Winter and Jack Hawley, and they did a whole search of Libby's lineage at the library."

"And?"

"And they couldn't find any connection, or any evidence that those things ever happened. It's just an ancient pirate's tale. Hawley never threatened to destroy the town, and Abby never offered herself up as a sacrifice. Hell, the whole thing's downright silly, if you think about it long enough."

"Maybe that's my problem. Maybe I haven't thought about it long enough."

Something flickered in Carl Bradford's eyes. He wasn't quite angry, but he was getting there. "What's your interest in all this?" he snapped.

"I'm thinking about resurrecting the old legend and turning it into a promotional event for The Seaside guests."

His look of great skepticism changed to a derisive sneer. "I sincerely doubt that," he said, fairly spitting the words.

"And I doubt your account of Abby Winter and Jack Hawley."

His jaw pulsed. Mayor Bradford was getting worked up, so I shrugged the rope off my shoulder and worked it in my hands a minute. He watched me do that, and it seemed to settle him down. He took a deep breath and said, "I told you about the search at the library."

"You did."

"It was quite exhaustive."

"I'm sure it was."

"Then what's your problem?"

"I wouldn't expect the library records to go back that far."

Mayor Bradford looked exasperated. "Then why are you bringing this up?"

"Because I think there's a better place to search for old records."

"You do."

"Uh huh."

"And where might that be?"

"The old churches around town."

He paused a long time before saying, "Any in particular?"

"Maybe I'll start with the one on Eighth and A1A."

23.

I LEFT A very jittery Mayor Bradford and headed across the courtyard, where I expected to find Rachel sitting in our rental car. I circled the entire building, and noticed a dozen empty parking spaces, but couldn't spot Rachel or the car in any of them. I pressed a key on my cell phone. Rachel answered with a whisper. "I can't talk right now."

"Where are you?" I said.

"What do you mean?"

"I'm done with the mayor. Your car's not here."

"I had to run an errand. I'll be there soon."

"An errand?"

"A girly thing. I don't want to talk about it."

"So where are you? And why are you whispering?"

"I'll be there in a few minutes. Find a diner on Main Street near the court house and grab a cup of coffee. I'll catch up with you in a few minutes and we can do the pirate thing together."

Rachel was right in thinking there'd be a diner near the court house. The one I entered a half-block away was nearly empty when I got there. That seemed reasonable, since most of the downtown workers would want to be back at their jobs by one o'clock. I checked my watch: 1:35pm. Rachel had said she'd be back "in a few minutes," but she'd invoked the dreaded "girly thing," which meant she was operating on Rachel time.

I picked out a corner booth that overlooked Main Street and pulled a menu from behind the old-fashioned sugar shaker. Opening it, my eyes went straight to the Shoo Fly Pie, which, being a pie of Pennsylvania origin, I planned to order in Libby Vail's honor.

The few customers who were still in the diner were paying their checks, so I expected the waitress would be along to take my order soon. In all probability, the pie I'd be served in St. Alban's would have crumbs mixed into the filling and topping, which is the Southern version. And that would be no problem, since that's the one I prefer.

Only I didn't get my pie.

By the time the last customer left, the waitress and cook were gone as well.

And I was alone in the diner.

Two minutes later I saw them: the gangster wannabes from the car that first night, when Rachel and I were headed back to The Seaside after our fight. I'd seen one of them, to be precise, but I knew the others would be hiding nearby. Finding myself in this situation, out of the blue, told me that Mayor Bradford was not only in on it, he was trying to protect it.

I put the menu back in its original spot, unraveled my rope, and walked to the next booth and tied one end to the metal post that held the table in place. Then I threaded the rope around the outside of the booth and kept it tucked against the floor. I reclaimed my seat and tied the other end to my right ankle. When they came for me I'd maintain eye contact, and keep my hands on the table. Entering the booth, they'd be studying my face or hands and weren't likely to notice the rope. Now all that was left to do was remove my switchblade from my boot, tuck it under my right knee, and wait for the dance to start.

There's a rhythm to these things, and I don't care if you're in Waco, LA, South Jersey or St. Alban's, it all goes down pretty much the same way. There are always two goons, tough guys. One comes at you from the front, the other hides in the kitchen or bathroom. The first goon forces you into the kitchen or bathroom so his buddy can hit you over the head as you enter, or pin your arms behind you while the first guy roughs you up. If there are three of them, one keeps watch while the others do their thing.

In this case there'd be four goons, though the pot-head driver and the kid with the piece-of-shit pistol were basically worthless. The guy riding shotgun would have some enforcement experience, and the dead-eyed guy in the back, the leader, would be dangerous. These two would provide the muscle. Working in my favor was the fact that I'd already disrespected them to their faces. They knew I wasn't afraid of them, so that would give them pause. Since I was either crazy or dangerous, they'd want to work up some courage before making their move. The two tough guys would come to my table and sit across from me while the others guarded the entrance and exit. We'd chat a minute at my booth while they made threats and showed me how tough they were. They'd pretend it was just a warning, but when I tried to get up from the table, they'd attack. They'd come at me savagely, inside the restaurant, because the place was deserted and my ability to move around would be hampered by the close quarters.

They had no reason to know I prefer fighting in close quarters.

On the other hand, this type of situation could go south in a hurry if I became distracted, and there was one unknown, one random element of the equation that could turn the whole encounter upside down.

Rachel.

Rachel was out there somewhere. She'd claimed to be on her way, but I suspected that whatever she was up to, it was going to be a while before she showed up. I hoped I was right, because these guys were moving so slow I was starting to get annoyed.

Okay, decision time. I had two options: stay or leave. If I hurried, I could still get out the front door before they had time to take up their positions. They weren't likely to attack me on Main Street in the middle of the day, so I could leave and avoid being attacked, protect Rachel by keeping her safely out of the line of fire, and deal with the gang-bangers another time.

That option sounded good except for one thing: if I ran away I wouldn't learn what they're hoping to gain. I already knew who sent them (the mayor) and I knew why (I'd threatened to check out the church). I suspected Libby Vail was being held prisoner in the church, or had been at one time. But I didn't know who was involved, or why. Usually when an elected official relies on gang-bangers, there are drugs involved. But I hadn't threatened anyone's drug trade.

I'd mentioned the local economy being boosted by the monthly celebrations honoring Libby Vail. Even The Seaside was thriving now—maybe it was because of me, but maybe I was part of something bigger, and if that was the case, I wanted to know what it was. While the rest of the nation struggled with business closings and high unemployment, St. Alban's seemed to be growing. Indeed, the whole town seemed to be riding a Kool-Aid high. So this encounter at the diner with the gang-bangers wasn't about drugs. It was about Libby Vail. Were they here to chase me out of town?

Beat me up for asking questions? Force me to stay away from the old church records? Kill me in cold blood?

I had to know.

But I was getting tired of waiting.

24.

IT DIDN'T GO down the way I thought it would.

I figured the two tough guys would overlook the rope, climb in the booth, and start threatening me. While they talked, I'd work my right hand down to the rope around my ankle, get it into my lap, switch hands, loop the rope around the highest part of the base of my table, and, when I stood to leave, I'd pull the rope tight with my left arm to trap them in the booth. By then the switchblade in my right hand would be open and I'd slit their throats before they had time to react. I'd go in the kitchen, avoid the pot-head's attack, and kill him quietly. Then I'd decide whether to kill the kid out front or just make my escape. I'd probably just go, unless he spotted me and tried to stop me.

That was the plan, and I thought it was a good one.

Only like I said, it didn't go down that way.

I was right in thinking the gang-bangers would come in the diner. But I didn't realize they'd come in the diner with the Sheriff and three deputies, all of whom held shotguns aimed at my face. They fanned out to give themselves a clean shot and limit any damage I might be able to do.

"Keep your hands on the table," the Sheriff said, "and without moving them from the table, get slowly to your feet."

I did as he said, and the shotguns moved to within five feet of me.

"He's got a blade on the seat," a deputy said.

The Sheriff moved in for a closer look.

"Why'd you tie yourself up?" he said.

The gang-bangers and two of the deputies started laughing, the rest of us kept still. The Sheriff got to one knee and slowly reached for my switchblade. Once he had it, he backed away, stood, and tossed a pair of handcuffs on the table.

"Put these on your wrists, but keep your elbows on the table the whole time," he said.

When I'd done that, he told me to stand and ease my way out of the booth slowly. Then, with the shotguns surrounding me, the Sheriff fitted me with leg cuffs, and secured them to my handcuffs with a chain.

They shuffled me out to a police van and closed the door. The deputy who hadn't laughed at me in the diner climbed behind the wheel, and the Sheriff rode shotgun.

Literally.

They took me south on A1A, a few miles past Amelia Island Plantation, and turned into the scrub area surrounding a gravel road that had been virtually invisible from the highway. The car slowed and dipped and I noticed a sign that said, "Site of the Little River Crossing, 1684–1758." Just as quickly, the front of the car raised and I guessed we'd crossed the river that used to be there.

No one was talking, but I wanted to plant a seed in their heads. I said, "Killing me might prove harder than you think."

They remained silent and stared straight ahead as they drove through the thickets and pine knobs. When they got to the base of a huge sand dune, the deputy put the wagon in park and the Sheriff turned around in his seat and looked at me.

"We got a problem," he said.

"Want to talk it out?" I said.

The Sheriff was a balding man, barrel-chested, powerfully built. He had pale-blue eyes and looked like he might have wrestled in college.

"How much do you know about the history of St. Alban's?" he said.

"Depends on how far back you want to go."

"Tell me what you think happened here three hundred years ago."

"Ah," I said.

25.

EVERYTHING I KNEW about what happened in St. Alban's three hundred years ago came from thirty minutes of online research. But it was enough to get me cuffed and shackled and locked in the back of a bulletproof paddy wagon guarded by two shotgun-wielding law enforcement officers.

"From what I understand," I said, "Gentleman Jack Hawley, the pirate, used to terrorize these shores in the early 1700s. He traveled with fifty men, seasoned fighters all, and had a sort of gentleman's agreement with the town of St. Alban's."

I waited for the Sheriff to acknowledge me. "Go on," he said.

"Hawley and his men agreed that whenever they came to St. Alban's, they would confine their activities to the one-block area surrounding the saloon. That area included a blacksmith, a leather shop, a clothing store, three whorehouses, two restaurants and a hotel."

"It did?"

I laughed. "How the hell do I know?"

The deputy laughed. "Sounded like you knew," he said.

"Why don't we go outside, sit on one of the sand dunes while I tell the story," I said, innocently.

"This is fine right here," the Sheriff said. "Keep talking."

"It makes sense there'd be whorehouses and restaurants

and a place to sleep," the deputy said.

"Percy," the Sheriff said. "Pipe down and let Creed tell his story."

Percy nodded. I said, "In return for not looting the town or harassing their womenfolk, the people of St. Alban's gave Hawley and his men refuge from the Governor of Florida and the British Navy."

"And then one day," the Sheriff prodded.

"And then one day the Governor of Florida offered a reward: one hundred pounds for the capture of Jack Hawley, and twenty pounds for each of his men. The people of St. Alban's conspired to capture Hawley and his crew while they were on shore leave and claim the reward. They enlisted the help of some soldiers from Amelia Island, but Hawley somehow learned about the scheme, and quelled the land attack. Then his ship was attacked at sea by the governor's navy, but Hawley's crew defeated them as well. After the battle, Hawley pointed his cannons at the town of St. Alban's and threatened to decimate it."

"Those were our forefathers," Percy said, and the Sheriff nodded. We all sat quiet for a few minutes, putting ourselves back in time. Finally the Sheriff said, "You know the rest? Why Hawley spared the town?"

"I know the legend," I said. "A teenager named Abby Winter offered to give herself to Hawley if he agreed to spare the town."

"Prettiest girl in town," Percy said.

Sheriff said, "And he took her up on it."

I said, "Hawley kept his word, and that's how he got the name Gentleman Jack Hawley."

Sheriff said, "I think he got the name because of the gentleman's agreement he had with the town before that incident."

I said, "Well, whatever."

The Sheriff said, "The point is, the town carried the guilt of Abby's sacrifice for the next three hundred years."

"Three hundred years of bad luck," Percy added.

"Which brings us to present day," I said.

"Which is why we're sitting in the scrub with a major problem," the Sheriff said. "Any idea what that problem might be?"

"I've got a good idea," I said.

"Thought you might. But let's hear you say it."

"I think the people of St. Alban's decided to change their luck about a year ago."

"How's that?" Percy said.

"A girl named Libby Vail happened to mention on TV that she was a direct descendant of Jack Hawley the pirate. Someone in St. Alban's heard about it, captured her, and a large part of the town is keeping her prisoner somewhere and using her disappearance to boost tourism."

"Well, that ain't exactly true," Percy said. He waited to see if his boss would shush him, but the Sheriff seemed lost in his thoughts. Percy added, "The thing is, the town was cursed. Hawley cursed the town, and it required the blood of his blood to reverse the curse. The tourism thing is just a side benefit."

"So you would have kidnapped her anyway?"

"Those that did would have."

"And you support it."

"Wouldn't expect you to understand," Percy said.

"Is the whole town in on it?"

The sheriff said, "The descendants are. Percy and I are descendants. The other deputies don't know."

"What about the gang-bangers in the diner?"

"They aren't our blood."

"Then why were you working with them?"

Percy laughed. "We aren't working with them. We were protecting them. From you!"

I looked at the Sheriff. "You know who I am?"

"Ran a check on you."

"You found me through a police check?"

"Not exactly. When we ran the check a guy named Darwin got in touch."

I smiled. Darwin is my Homeland Security boss, my facilitator.

The Sheriff continued. "According to Darwin, you could buy this whole town. Or kill it, if you wanted to."

"And you believe him?"

"Got no reason to believe him, or not to. And don't care to find out either way."

"How many of you are descendants?"

The Sheriff and Percy looked at each other. Sheriff said, "What, eighty?"

"Maybe eighty," Percy said.

"And you're keeping her in the old church on the corner of Eighth and A1A?"

They looked at each other again. "Told you he knew," the Sheriff said.

"How do you keep her quiet during the church services," I said. "Drug her?"

"What? Are you nuts? What kind of man would drug a young woman?"

A guy like me, I thought, since I planned to drug Rachel that very night if I survived.

"Can I ask you something?" I said.

135

The Sheriff shrugged. "Don't see what difference it makes at this point."

"I've noticed a disproportionate number of people in town are almost insanely happy, including you guys. Why's that?"

"We're grateful for Libby's sacrifice."

"Sacrifice?"

"Uh huh."

"Are you kidding me? Abby Winter made a sacrifice. Libby Vail was kidnapped. Hell of a difference!"

The Sheriff gave me a curious look. "You think we're *forcing* her to stay?"

"Aren't you?"

26.

CONVINCED I WASN'T going to kill them, Percy removed my chains. Convinced they were going to remove my chains, I decided not to kill them.

The Sheriff put his shotgun down and said, "Libby's not our prisoner, but there is a conspiracy of sorts."

He paused as if trying to find the best words.

"A bunch of us—the descendants—are helping her hide here."

"So eighty people are working together?"

"Maybe eighty."

"And you've managed to keep it a secret this whole time?"

"Till you showed up."

"How's it possible for that many people to keep a secret?"

"We're all related."

"What's she up to, that requires such secrecy?"

The Sheriff and Percy exchanged a look.

I dove in. "It's the healing power, isn't it?"

Percy said, "Told you he knew. That's why he was at the church, trying to talk to the elders."

I said, "I felt something myself and was trying to find out what it was. These old people were like statues at first, and then they started moving around. There were two guys in the van watching them. The driver made a phone call and you showed up in seconds. How'd you get there so fast?"

"We were already nearby, north on A1A."

"Guarding Libby?"

"Guarding her secret and making sure the elders got to her safely. We sometimes help with the driving."

"Tell me about the elders," I said.

"Libby's not a healer," the Sheriff said, "but she has the power to make people feel better. We're her people, and she's our blood. Of the roughly eighty descendants, there are fifteen or twenty older ones. Some are sick, some arthritic. When she's at the church, if we think it's safe, we bring them to see her. If we're not sure, we bring them to the churchyard so they can be close enough for her to ease their pain."

"And you believe this."

"Doesn't matter if I believe it."

"Why's that?"

"'Cause *you* do."

Ignoring him, I said, "And where does Beth fit into all this?"

"Beth is one of us."

"Why hasn't she had any luck?"

"Luck?"

"Well, it seems the whole town is prospering, but Beth's husband died, she's losing money, her B&B's falling apart..."

"Libby doesn't bring good luck, she attracts good people."

I thought about that a minute.

"Like Dr. Carstairs?"

"Surely you've wondered how a rinky-dink town like ours could land a nationally respected medical guy like Carstairs."

"You don't think his coming here had anything to do with the climate, the beaches, the friendly people, the desire to do something simple but meaningful?"

"You tell me."

"What do you mean?"

"You're a six-billion-dollar caretaker and part-time cook. Your girlfriend's a twenty-five-million dollar waitress. You telling me you folks always had a desire to do something simple but meaningful before you visited our little town?"

"So you think Libby Vail summoned us?"

"Nope."

"Then what?"

"She summoned you."

"What, Beth couldn't find her own cook and caretaker locally?"

Percy laughed. "He just don't get it, does he?"

"Get what?" I said.

"Libby summoned you for Beth."

"You mean—"

"You're going to marry Beth."

I laughed. "You're insane!"

"Maybe."

"I'm with Rachel."

"Uh huh."

"Beth and I haven't exchanged fifty words together."

"Not yet."

"Well, if she's got a thing for me, why hasn't she said so?"

"Wouldn't be proper, long as you've got a girlfriend."

"This whole thing is crazy. I'm not even attracted to Beth in that way."

"Libby won't let you feel it till the time is right."

"So you're saying that the reason Beth's good fortune lagged behind the town's is that she was waiting on me to show up?"

"She probably didn't know it was you at first, but when you agreed to take care of the B&B she probably figured

139

it out."

"So Libby's not only got the power to ease people's pain, she's also a matchmaker?"

"Ain't it the same thing?"

27.

THE SHERIFF CALLED Beth and told her I knew all about Libby. I couldn't hear her part of the conversation, but his included "It's not your fault," and "No, it's okay," and "I don't see that we have any other choice but to trust him," and "If you don't mind, I'd like you to take him," and "Right."

When he hung up I asked him what that was all about.

"Beth is going to take you to see Libby, so you can see for yourself that everything's okay."

"When?"

"Tonight."

"What about Rachel?"

"We'd prefer to keep a lid on this, as long as Libby's willing to stay in town."

"I've mentioned my theories to Rachel."

"She believe you?"

"She thinks I'm nuts."

"Well then, it's your call, but if Rachel doesn't need to know…"

I saw where this was going.

"You're hoping I'll see Libby, realize she's here of her own free will, put the whole thing behind me and keep my mouth shut."

"I'm counting on it."

"And if I don't?"

The Sheriff sighed. "We're peaceful, small-town people. We don't make threats or kill people who get in our way. When Curly Bradford couldn't get me to run you out of town, he did a stupid thing and called the only violent people he knew."

"And you stepped in and saved their lives," I said.

"Part of my job description," he said.

"To protect and serve?"

We both smiled. I liked the Sheriff, liked Percy too. But I wasn't going to allow the town to hold a girl hostage. I'd been through this before. A few years back my best friend captured a girl and kept her locked up in his safe room for three years. He did it out of love, and the fear of losing her forever. But I couldn't let that continue, either.

The Sheriff said, "Libby has the power to help people and wants to. And you have the power to take her away from us, get us in a heap of trouble with the FBI, and make our town a laughing stock. So yes, I'm hoping she'll be able to convince you to help us."

"Help you keep her secret?"

"Help us protect her."

"And hide her?"

"That too."

Percy drove us to The Seaside, where I found Rachel pacing the porch waiting for me. But when she saw me enter the driveway with the police she didn't run over and hug me as I would have expected. Instead, she stared wide-eyed at the Sheriff and Percy until they were out of sight. Crazy as it sounds, I had the distinct feeling she thought we might have come to arrest her for something. Of course, with Rachel you never know what's going on in her mind. She might have been thinking about Easter Eggs.

"I heard they arrested you!" she said. "I'm so sorry I wasn't there to pick you up!"

"It's okay."

"What did they do to you? Why didn't you call?"

"Come inside, I'll tell you everything."

The Sheriff had already called Beth, so she and I sat down with Rachel. We'd gotten about halfway through the explanation when The Seaside's phone rang. Beth took the call and after a few seconds, passed it off to me. I listened for a minute, asked a few questions, listened some more, and then hung up.

Rachel said, "Who was that?"

"Dr. Carstairs. He called about D'Augie."

Rachel jumped to her feet. It was interesting to watch how her eyes lit up. "How is he?"

"He's dead."

Rachel's knees buckled. She made an attempt to grab the arm of the love seat, but missed. She hit the floor before I could get to her.

"I'll get a wet cloth and smelling salts," Beth said, moving out of the room quickly.

I got Rachel up on the couch and elevated her torso. The salts worked. Beth handed me the towel, and I dabbed at Rachel's face. When she came to she began flailing. It took a minute, then she was better.

"Is it true?" she sobbed. "D'Augie's dead?"

"I'm sorry. I know you liked him."

"What happened?"

"They're not sure. He may have had a reaction to the antibiotic they administered for the burns. They never got a proper medical history on him, so they had no way of knowing."

"Oh, my God!" she wailed. "Poor D'Augie." She was

inconsolable. So much so that I began to wonder if her interest in him could have been more than casual. On the other hand, her initial reaction was bogus. I'd seen enough fainters in my life to know that Rachel was faking it. But why?

Under normal circumstances I would have stayed home to help her work through her grief. But I had a date with Beth that couldn't wait, so I gave Rachel a double sedative and tucked her in for the night.

It crossed my mind that I could be walking into an ambush at the church. But it didn't feel like one, because Beth would be with me, and surely the Sheriff knew how easily I could turn things around by putting a knife to her neck if I needed to get away. While I didn't think it was an ambush, I didn't know what I might encounter when I got there, so I took the time to hide some light weapons and tools in my warm-up jacket and pants. I opened my little leather kit, the one where I stored various tools of my trade, such as syringes and opiates and poisons and…

And noticed a vial was missing.

I shook Rachel until she opened her eyes. "Wh-What?" she stammered, deep in a fog.

I held the kit in front of her face and made her focus on it. "Rachel, listen to me. There was a small vial in here that I told you never to touch. It's one of the deadliest poisons in the world." I shook her again. "Rachel!" I said, and slapped her across the face. Her eyes opened to about half-mast and a crooked smile formed on her lips. When she spoke her voice had a sing-song lilt to it.

"You said he was trying to kill you," she said.

"What?"

"He loved the Red Drink," she said.

"You poisoned D'Augie?"

144

She giggled, as if laughing in her sleep. "D'Augie said Red Drink was to die for!" She drifted off again.

I pinched her nostrils shut till she started to choke. I shouted her name, and she gagged and shook her head. "Leave me alone!" she said, while trying to slap me away.

"Who was he?"

"Huh?"

"Who was D'Augie?"

"Huh? Oh. I dunno."

"Why did he want to kill me?"

"I dunnooo."

"Did he tell you anything about himself?"

"Huh?"

I shook her again and repeated the question. She tried to swat me with her hand.

"I'm serious, Rachel. Tell me what he said."

"Just that he was named after his father and his father's best friend."

"His father's name was Augie?"

"No. Augustus."

I felt as though someone had drilled a hole in my chest.

"Dunno what the D was for," she murmured.

The room seemed to swirl around me. I tucked Rachel in again and let her sleep. I didn't have to ask her anything else. I knew exactly who the kid was, though I'd never known of his existence before that moment. D'Augie was named after his father, Augustus, and his father's best friend, Donovan Creed.

Donovan and Augustus: D'Augie.

Augustus Quinn had been my best friend for more than fifteen years. We'd killed together, worked together, and defended our country. He was a monster of a man, born with a rare disease that misshaped his head and facial features. About four years ago Augustus had fallen in love with a young con artist named Alison, whom I'd recruited to work for my agency at Homeland. Around that time I had a medical issue that put me in a coma for three years. When I recovered, I learned that Augustus had kidnapped Alison and was keeping her in a concrete cell in his warehouse in Philadelphia. It's a long story, but in order to rescue Alison I had to kill my best friend.

Fuck.

Augustus never told me he had a son.

Life's crazy sometimes, you know?

Wow.

Ah well, fuck it.

I mean, there's nothing I can do about it now, right?

Nothing to do but close that chapter of my life and move on.

28.

THE LAND AROUND the little church was flat, the lot surrounded by pines. The church was two stories high, made entirely of flagstone, except for the corrugated red metal roofing, the wooden door, and the windows. There was a slate floor standing area in front of the church that was maybe twenty feet wide and twelve feet deep. To the right of the church were two flagstone columns that stood about fifteen feet high. The columns were connected at the top by a limestone cap. A few inches below the cap an old, cast-iron bell hung from a wooden beam. The rope for the bell clapper was long enough to reach the ground, but was tied off to a cleat so children couldn't reach it.

We parked Beth's car in the gravel area on the left side, and from that angle I could see a wooden balcony that extended from a small gable. Before exiting the car, Beth put her hand on my wrist, very gently. I looked down at it, and then raised my eyes to her face. She held my gaze a moment, then closed her eyes. I leaned over and lightly kissed her lips. She didn't kiss me back.

I kissed her again, and this time she opened her eyes and returned the kiss. I started moving closer, eager for more, but she said, "It's not our time yet."

"Are you sure?" I said. "Because to me, it really feels like it's our time."

She smiled and lifted her hand from my wrist, and placed it to my face. I'd never felt so much energy from a person's touch before, not even Kathleen Chapman, who I almost married.

"We're meant to be, and it will happen, but it's not our time yet."

"Can I have just fifteen minutes of it now with you, across the street, on the beach?"

She did that adorable pouty thing she sometimes did with her mouth, then sighed and said, "I'm not ready yet, and you're not ready. But when it's our time, you won't be disappointed. I promise."

"A rain check then."

"Let's call it a heart check," she said, placing her palm on my heart.

I looked past her, through her window, thinking of that gorgeous, deserted beach a scant two minutes away. "How about a quick ten minutes now, and when we're both ready, we can deduct it from eternity?"

"You drive a hard bargain," she said, "but no."

"Well, you've certainly put me off my game." I kissed her hand and we climbed out of the car. The second-floor balcony above us looked to be about two feet deep, was covered, and appeared to be decorative. But once inside the church, I saw that it was attached to a small, hidden gable about six feet wide and eight feet deep. You reach that little room by descending into a trapdoor about four feet below the ante way and then crawling some twenty feet under the chapel until you reach a wooden ladder. That twenty-foot crawl behind Beth was the toughest of my life. Being that close to her backside would have killed a lesser man. When we got to the ladder we climbed fifteen feet to a landing. Beyond the thick, locked, wooden door, stood the little gable room where I met Libby Vail.

Libby was thin, but appeared healthy. She was sitting on a window box, surrounded by stacks of old, moldy books and parchment.

"Hey Beth!" she said, brightly.

"Hi Libby. This is Donovan Creed."

Libby and Beth exchanged a knowing smile that was so obvious it almost embarrassed me. Beth blushed and lowered her eyes and cleared a small space on the window box and sat there. It happened to be the only place one could sit in the cramped little area.

"Hello, Mr. Creed."

I cocked my head to one side. "I notice you're missing a fingernail on your right index digit."

Libby laughed. "Do you always start conversations this way?"

"I do. Always."

She turned to Beth. "See? I told you he'd be funny!" To me, she said, "Seriously, why do you ask?"

"I found it in the picnic basket Beth brought you one day. I figured you broke it when you scratched your initials on the bottom of the basket."

Beth looked at her curiously. Libby thought a moment, then said, "Oh. I think that must have happened the night I was trying to channel Jack Hawley. I kept scratching my initials while saying my name."

"Why?"

She looked at me sheepishly. "I was hoping to somehow cross the space-time continuum, like they talk about in the movies. Maybe get him to send me a clue of some sort. Crazy, I know, but wow, you're really good. I mean, to find a fingernail and scratch marks and put all this together? I'm impressed."

Impressed or not, I had to ask the question, in spite of Beth.

"Are you being held here against your will?"

Libby laughed, heartily. "No, of course not. If I were, I could just open the door to the balcony and call for help."

I gestured at the tiny room, "Then what are you doing? Your parents and friends have been mourning you for nearly a year. The FBI came down…"

Libby held up a hand. "Please. Don't make me feel guilty, I know all that. I'm just giving back. Some people join the Peace Corps, I hide in a church."

"Except that your loved ones would know if you were in the Peace Corps."

"I won't be here much longer."

"You stay in this cramped room all the time?"

"It's more like a home base. I stay with different friends at different times. There's a schedule, but yes, I sleep here sometimes, and this is where I conduct my research."

"What are you researching?"

She gestured to the books and parchment paper. "The local churches and library have opened all their books to me. I've spent the past year filling in the details of my heritage. When I'm not reading, when the church is locked, I wander around the building. And when my friends come to visit, we go for walks. Beth and some of the day ladies drive me to parks or deserted parts of the beach. It's easy not to be recognized if I'm wearing a wig and trying to blend in. Sometimes a group of us go fishing." She pointed to a laptop. "Plus, I've got all the modern conveniences, iPod, iTouch, computer, TV…"

"I've heard some bullshit in my day," I said, "but this takes the cake."

She eyed me, curiously. "You don't believe I'm here for historical reasons?"

"Absolutely not."

"Why's that?"

I picked up one of the maps. "This is a terrain map." I gestured to some sheets she'd tacked to the wall. "And those look a lot like geological surveys."

"So?"

"So you might be researching your family history, but there's more to it. Otherwise you wouldn't need to keep your presence quiet."

She said nothing.

Beth watched me with a tender light in her eyes that made me feel particularly good.

And then it hit me.

"You're searching for treasure!"

She seemed about to protest, then saw my smug smile and gave up. She offered a smile of her own and said, "Wouldn't you search for treasure if you were me? If you thought you could find it?"

"I would indeed." I paused a moment. Then asked, "So, did you find it?"

She shook her head sadly. "Nope. All this effort, and not so much as a doubloon. We gave up months ago. We thought that by traveling around the island I might be able to sense Jack's presence. But either I never got to the right place, or we were wrong."

"We?"

"The original descendants and me."

"No one kidnapped you?"

"Nope."

"The eighty descendants have been hiding you, driving you

151

around, trying to help you find pirate treasure?"

"At first."

"No treasure?"

"Not a scrap."

"Then why stick around?"

"Because the people around here have become my friends, and they need me. Every day different people, descendants of the original settlers, drove me around the island while I tried to pick up some sort of cosmic connection to Jack Hawley. The closest I ever came to getting a feeling was right here, in this old church." She absently touched the necklace around her neck. "But Jack couldn't have buried anything here. It was a highly visible location in his era, and the church wasn't built until ten years after his death."

"That's interesting, but you haven't answered my question."

"Why am I still here if there's no treasure?"

"That's the one."

Libby shrugged her shoulders and gave me a "you're not going to believe me" sort of smile. She said, "You're not going to believe me, but whenever I'd be somewhere more than an hour, people started showing up. They said being near me made them feel better. So I love the area, love the people, and they need me. I go to the hospital every night, and the nursing home, and walk through the halls. If someone is particularly ill I go in and sit with them a few minutes."

I thought about how I tried to find her at the church that morning before dawn, and how I'd felt the power near the hospital, before it faded away.

"Can I ask where you were just before dawn this morning?"

"I went to the hospital to visit Jimbo Pimm's grandfather."

152

"Because?"

"He's a cancer patient. He'd been at Savannah Memorial, but they sent him home to die last week. He took a turn for the worse in the middle of the night and Jimbo brought him to the hospital. While they worked on him, Jimbo came and asked if I might be able to help."

"Did you?"

"Did I go? Yes, Jimbo drove me."

"Did it help?"

"No. I mean, I can't cure people, but he said I took away his pain. I hear that a lot, and do what I can, but it doesn't last. I told him I'd sit with him again tonight, for an hour."

I didn't believe for a minute she had healing powers, but I couldn't dispute the fact that something was going on. I'd seen what happened to the old people in the churchyard. And there was no question that my mood elevated when I was around her. The room we were in was only five feet tall and I'd been stooping long enough to know my back should be stiff, and yet I felt not the slightest pain. I decided Libby must have something about her that altered people's perception of pain when they were physically near her. I didn't want to feel any pain later on, so I sat on the floor.

"Why can't you go public?" I said. "If this gift is real, you could help millions of people."

"I have empathy for everyone in pain. But if word got out about me, my life would be a mess. I mean, would you want half the world coming to your door and the other half trying to perform experiments on you?"

She had a point, but who doesn't? As far as I was concerned, this thing was wrapped up. Normally I would have climbed back down the ladder by now and gone home. A shot of bourbon might have been in order. But here I sat. I knew why, I just didn't want to admit it. See, I don't believe in healers, and yet I knew the only reason I kept sitting there was because I felt so damned good sitting there. I had no aches or pains and my mind was soaring. I felt better than I had since I was a kid, running over the grass in my bare feet, a light breeze on my forehead, lots of friends…

"I bet you could get laid anytime you want," I said, in my semi-dream state.

"Excuse me?"

Beth and Libby were staring at me.

"What I meant to say was how long do you intend to stay here?"

She looked at Beth and shrugged. "I promised I'd do a year. But I can't very well pop out on the exact anniversary, can I? So I'll probably hang out a few more months."

I gestured toward the clutter that surrounded her. "Find anything interesting in those old church records?"

"Oh, yes, indeed."

"Such as?"

"Well, for one thing, there was a midwife who gave birth in 1711 to a little girl named Libby Vail."

"Spelled the same way?"

"Uh huh."

"Now there's a coincidence! Who were the parents?"

"Henry and Johanna Ames."

"Oh, too bad. I suppose Libby Vail must have been a popular name back in those days."

She looked at me and smiled. "Right."

"I mean, even today there's probably, what, five thousand Libby Vails walking around?"

"Try four."

"Four?"

She fidgeted with her necklace again and said, "I did an internet search. There are exactly four of us in the whole United States."

The thin gold chain around Libby's neck looked new. The pendant attached to it was an old circular piece of metal with what appeared to be ancient etching.

"Tell me about the necklace," I said.

"I found it when digging in the crawl space my first day here. I went right to it, was drawn to it the minute we turned the corner. It's quite old, but there's no connection to Jack Hawley. Unless he loved playing rugby!"

She removed the necklace and handed it to me. On one side someone had scratched the words, "I Love." On the other: "Rugby."

"How old is this?"

"It's old, at least two hundred years. But it couldn't date to Jack Hawley's time. I know, because I researched the sport and no one called it Rugby before 1750."

"Whatever happened to Hawley?"

"He was captured and hanged on March 25, 1711."

"You're positive?"

"One hundred percent."

I thought about how I had faked my death a couple of times, and said, "How can you be so sure?"

"Two sailors joined Hawley's crew when they were on shore leave in Charleston, South Carolina. They turned Jack in to the authorities after watching him command the ship for an entire month."

"How do you know he didn't bury his treasure in Charleston?"

"Because, according to the traitors, he never left the ship in Charleston. They captured him in St. Alban's, trying to buy produce for a voyage to Jamaica."

"Any witnesses at the trial?"

"His best friends, George and Marie Stout, were forced to testify. Under protest, they identified Jack and admitted he used to paddle up the Little River and dock at their place. Their kids said Jack spent a lot of time there."

"And you searched that area?"

"Every square inch. I thought I had it made when I discovered an old well on the actual tract that belonged to the Stouts. But I got nothing in the way of a vibe."

We sat silently for a few minutes. Then I said, "How do you plan to explain your disappearance?"

"When I'm ready to rejoin society I'll have someone drive me halfway across the country and drop me off in the woods near a city. I'll wander into town and say I've been kidnapped, blindfolded, and moved around so much I don't know where I've been all this time. They'll ask loads of questions, and I'll get a few things mixed up, but if I didn't, it wouldn't make sense, right?"

"The deputy said you were kidnapped."

"Figuratively, not literally. When the descendants came and talked to me I thought they were crazy, but I promised to think about it. That night, alone in my dorm room, I started whispering my name while thinking about Hawley. And something happened. I know this will sound crazy to you, but I *felt* him speak my name. Over the next few months it happened several times."

"You're right, it does sound crazy."

"Told you."

"Any history of insanity in your family?"

"None that I've found, and believe me, I've looked!"

"So it started as a treasure hunt, and now you're helping

people. If you want the big bucks, why not do a reality show on TV and make millions?"

"As I said, I don't want my life to be a circus. Plus, I'm deep into my research, and things I've dismissed before are starting to make sense to me."

"Like what?"

She seemed to glow, caught up in the moment. "I think I'm onto something even more valuable than money."

"What's that?"

"The secret of my heritage."

"Meaning?"

"We're all a product of our heritage, Mr. Creed."

"And why is that so important?"

She smiled. "Well, I'm descended from a famous pirate."

"Jack Hawley."

"Yes, *Gentleman* Jack, as he liked to be called. And about three hundred years ago—"

It was my turn to hold up a hand. "I know the story."

Libby's eyes sparkled. "Oh, no, you don't."

"I do."

"Sorry, but you don't."

"Maybe not every detail," I conceded, "but I think I've got a pretty good handle on it."

"Trust me," she said. "You have no idea."

"I think I do," I said, stubbornly.

She flashed a mischievous grin. "Do you?" she said. A little giggle escaped from her throat. "Do you?" she said, louder, and as she said it her giggle grew until it burst through the tiny room and echoed off the walls.

PART TWO

THEN

1.

THE YEAR OF Our Lord, 1710...

The ship was huge.

With three masts, twenty-eight guns, and a crew of fifty-seven men, it carried a cargo of sugar cane, medicine, wild pigs, and Jamaican rum. Though it pushed more than three hundred tons, it fairly flew through the water. And such water it was! Pure and clean with a light-green hue, and when the bow slapped down, sending a light spray over the deck, it stung the eye and tasted warm and salty on the lips.

The ship was surrounded on all sides by sparkling emerald seas, far as the eye could see. Astern, a dozen porpoises frolicked in the wake, performing wild acrobatic jumps and gyrations to the amusement of the twenty-two hardened crewmen currently off duty. While sailors around the world considered it good luck to share their rations with the sleek sea creatures, it was a rare event to do so, since rations were typically meager and meant to last. But for this particular crew, these were bountiful times. With the ship's hold freshly restocked the day before, the men could finally afford to toss the last of their weevil-infested biscuits overboard.

Amid ships, a solitary man stood alone on the upper-deck bridge. Lean and tall he was, with long black hair and piercing blue eyes that sparkled when he laughed or had a story to tell. But there were no stories to be told today, for he was determined to ride this strong westerly wind as far as it would take them. He heard a fluttering sound, looked up at the sails, and frowned. Then he barked an order to the nervous helmsman.

The quartermaster, a stocky red-haired Welshman named Pim, tugged at his enormous fiery red mutton chops with both hands, as was his habit when annoyed. It was well known among the ship's crew that the angrier Pim became, the harder he pulled. He'd been tugging his beard with growing frequency this quarter-hour, and was in fact a mere tug away from physically assaulting his fellow crewman. The Captain's sharp word had probably saved the helmsman from a severe beating. Pim gave a nod of acknowledgment to the Captain before turning his attention to the tireless sailors who had been working the sails two hours non-stop, attempting to fill every inch of silk with wind. Up to now, they'd made great progress despite their semi-drunk helmsman's poor showing.

But the man's errant steering threatened to undermine morale.

The captain glared at his tipsy crew-member, and cocked his head as if to convey a final warning. The helmsman, sober enough to catch his meaning, immediately apologized to the quartermaster and sailors. It was a sincere apology and a wise decision on his part, considering the harsh penalties for drunkenness while under sail. In normal circumstances, when transporting cargo to port, a drunken helmsman would at the very least be treated to five lashes across the bare back with a rope dipped in tar. Had the infraction occurred under battle conditions, he would surely suffer death by keelhaul.

But neither captain nor crew were in a mood to punish anyone today. As the steering adjustment took effect, both the captain and Pim checked the sail before catching each other's eye. The captain winked, and Pim pumped his fist in the air and shouted to his sailors, "Keep 'er sheets full, lads! As big and full as the jugs of St. Alban's."

Roberts, the sharp-eyed lookout, shouted down from the crow's nest. "Aye, and which jugs would ye be referrin' to, Mr. Pim? Them that's filled with grog or them that's filled with milk?"

The crew members laughed lustily. Those who glanced in the captain's direction noticed a smile on his handsome face, and to a man, their spirits soared. This crew had worked on many ships, for many masters, but none had worked for a man like this. A frown from him was enough to shake their confidence, but his smile was like gold in their pockets. This was a captain who owned the hearts and minds of his crew, having earned his status the same way all pirate-ship captains wielded absolute authority over their vessels: by unanimous vote of the crew. True, he had proven himself a legendary strategist, loyal friend, and fierce fighter. But there was something more, some indefinable, mysterious quality that was difficult to pin down. The men couldn't explain it, but they felt more powerful in his presence. Less surly, more content. Crazy as it sounded when speaking of it to each other, they agreed that they could somehow *feel* his presence when he was within a mile's distance. More importantly, from the moment he'd stepped on board, their fortunes increased. Winds were stronger, storms fewer, and waters more peaceful and calm than ever before. There had been fewer injuries and illness, and the wounds that did occur healed faster. Even the food seemed to taste better when the captain was on board.

The captain had joined them two years ago. Now, after several campaigns at sea, he and his ship, *The Fortress*, had become well known throughout the Caribbean. No, more than that: they had achieved celebrity status.

The porpoises abruptly ended their show and darted ahead, providing escort for a league or so before finally peeling off in search of some alternate aquatic activity.

When *The Fortress* was under full sail, with a strong wind, she could cover a hundred miles in a day. But they wouldn't require a full day to reach Shark's Bay. At this speed, they'd have the captain dropped off there by mid-afternoon. As always, he'd change into commoner's clothes, lower an open boat into the water, and row it over the shoals, up the Little River to the edge of St. Alban's settlement to scope out the lay of the land. *The Fortress* would head back out to sea three miles, make a wide loop, and then double back to St. Alban's, to the deep water of North Port, off Sinner's Row, where she would finally anchor in sixty feet of water a quarter-mile out and wait for word from the captain that it was safe to go ashore.

Roberts spied a flock of seabirds, and the atmosphere above and below decks crackled with anticipation.

They continued heading due west, toward Shark's Bay. Though they sailed under the red, white and blue flag of the British East India Company, this was a pirate ship with a pirate crew.

It was Jack Hawley's ship, Jack Hawley's crew.

2.

THE STEADY BREEZE on St. Alban's Beach could not penetrate the gnarled trees and dense thickets three hundred yards inland where Abby Winter shared a wooden shanty house with her mother and stepfather. It was early afternoon on a cloudless day and the July heat was stifling. Abby and her mother had emptied the chamber pots that morning, but hadn't had time to properly clean them.

"Please don't do this," Abby said. "It's humiliating!"

"It's been decided, child, so let it be."

They weren't talking about chamber pots.

"It's posted for tomorrow," Abby said, "but posting doesn't make it mandatory. You're allowed to change your mind on matters such as these. People do it all the time without consequence."

"I could change my mind, but I will not. As I say, it's been decided."

Abby's mother, Hester, handed her one of the tarnished chamber pots. Abby accepted it and winced as the odor hit her nostrils. Her mother said, "Let's get these done before he thinks we're conjuring a demon."

Abby gasped. Her eyes made a quick sweep of the trees that ringed their shanty. She briefly wondered if her mother had gone daft. It was bad enough she'd agreed to the public posting, and now she was making witchery comments! Abby

165

scolded her mother with a severe whisper. "You cannot have said that!"

"Don't be so skittish, child. There's no one 'round."

"There's always someone around," Abby said. "The river crossing is just yonder. Pray, you must not speak of these things, even lightly."

"I'll say no more when you talk less of the posting."

"But this *must* be discussed! He's your husband, not your owner. He can't just *sell* you in the town square!"

Hester started to say something, but changed her mind. She looked at the stained chamber pot in her hand and sighed. Ten years earlier she'd been known throughout the colony for her beauty. Now, more often than not, her hair was a tangled mass of mud-soaked curls. She rubbed her shoulder absently and winced. A horrific fungus had taken over her right shoulder and begun a steady progression across her upper back. On hot days like this, her afflicted skin cracked open, releasing a milky liquid that stuck to the fibers of her fustian smock. Hester had to continually lift the fabric from her skin or risk forming a scab that would have to be torn away later.

Abby noticed her discomfort. "Has your condition worsened?"

Hester frowned. "Faith, child, I'm common indeed to suffer before you. What a sorry complainer I've become."

"You've become nothing of the sort, though I know not how you maintain your sanity. You've had a hard burden from the day we moved here."

"Not so hard compared to others," Hester said, making the sign of the cross on her chest. She looked around before whispering. "Know what I wish?"

"What?"

"That I could uncover my shoulder and back so the sun

could heal it."

"Surely you'd be seen and forced to bear the consequence."

"Aye, child."

The constant burning and itching was impossible to get used to, and had thus far eluded home remedy. Though her well-formed body continued to draw looks from the men of St. Alban's, Hester's face and neck had turned ash-gray from drinking a potion of colloidal silver forced upon her by her husband, and that, along with the heavy scar tissue framing her eyes, and her thrice-broken nose, added years to her appearance.

Hester studied Abby's face carefully before shaking her head. "Being sold to a new man is a way to better things for me."

"But—"

"You've seen my life, you know how he is."

"I *do* know," Abby said, gently. "But you could divorce him." She looked around to make sure he hadn't come up on them. He hadn't, but she whispered anyway. "You could divorce him and take me with you."

Hester laughed. "And how many women have you seen in North Florida Colony with money enough to divorce a husband? As for taking you with me, I cannot, as you're the purpose for the sale."

There was a slight delay before the horror registered in Abby's face. Hester softened her tone. "Abby," she said. "Look at you. Even in these conditions, you are far the fairest maid in the colony. I do not wish you to think ill of me, abandoning you to such a harsh man."

"Yet how can I not?"

"I have a plan."

"What plan?"

"He will show you a softer side. Of this I'm certain. You won't remember, but when he took us in, he was tolerant, even kind, at times. Of course, I was young and pretty then. These days I vex him constantly, with my limp, my face, and frailty."

"'Course I remember," Abby said. "It was only a few years past. But he's the one caused your limp! Your 'face and frailty,' as you put it, is a consequence of his constantly boxing your nose and eyes and cuffing your ears."

Hester dabbed at the light sheen of sweat on her forehead. "You'll understand when you're older."

"Truly? And what will I understand? How you let that swine of a man cuff you about and rut you day and night as if you were a crippled sow?"

Hester's eyes blazed for a brief moment, and Abby hoped to receive a sharp rebuke or slap across the face. Any such response would show that her mother retained a measure of spirit. But the fire in Hester's eyes quickly died, leaving behind only an apathetic stare. Instead of lashing out, she shrugged and said, "We suffer for our children, not ourselves."

Abby frowned. "And what is that presumed to mean?"

Hester turned and started walking toward the creek. Abby followed, waiting for a response. She watched her mother scoop a handful of sand from the water's edge and dump it in her chamber pot. Abby sighed, and did the same. They swirled the sand around the inside of the pots with their fingers, scrubbing and grinding it against the hardened fecal deposits. Then they rinsed the pots in the creek and inspected them.

Abby said, "Fine. Don't tell me. But why can we not just leave this wretched man and his poor excuse for a house?"

"Leave? Has your brain been seized by vipers? Where would you have us go, child, Sinner's Row?"

Abby knew her mother was right. There weren't many pleasant options for women in North Florida Colony in 1710. She lowered her eyes and said, "I like not the way he looks at me."

"He has looked at you that way for two full years, though you knew it not till now."

The way Hester proclaimed it gave Abby pause. "Two years ago I was thirteen!"

"Aye, child," Hester said. "Now ponder that fact a moment before speaking."

Abby did. In the colonies, as in Europe, the minimum legal age for marriage had been twelve for girls, fourteen for boys, for as long as anyone could remember. Still, in Abby's experience, it was outrageous to think of a forty-year-old man rutting a child. Then the weight of Hester's words hit her and made Abby realize for the first time what had transpired in the man's house. Her stomach lurched.

"You kept him from me these two years. That's why you accepted these many beatings and ruts. You were protecting me."

"Aye, child."

They embraced and held each other for a long moment. When they separated, Hester said, "It was not your fault I chose a surly man." Her free hand drifted absently to her face and touched the bumps at the bridge of her nose. "I did what I could to keep him off you these many months."

"But now?"

Hester fixed her gaze on Abby's eyes. "Now you're fifteen, fully bloomed, and his desire to have you exceeds my ability to protest."

Abby's eyes widened. "So I'm to be your way out? You're to have a new husband and I'm to be left here to rut the swine?"

"You're young and strong and untouched. He'll be nice to you for the duration."

Abby was so busy trying to wrap her mind around her circumstance, she almost missed it.

"What duration?"

"Walk with me, child."

They crossed the small clearing and stood close behind the privy, squinting their eyes against the foul odor. When she was absolutely certain her words would not be overheard, Hester whispered, "When Thomas Griffin buys me, I will set at once to acquire a vial of arsenic from his apothecary which I shall give to you. A few drops in your stepfather's every meal will do the devil's work within two months. And you will rise in station, inheriting his house and the proceeds of his business."

"You cannot be serious. I'd have to marry him for this to be the legal result."

"That may seem the worst part to you now, but on further reflection, you'll find it a sound plan to help you become a young woman of property."

Abby had no intention of reflecting thus. In fact, she had plans of her own, that she had never discussed with her mother. But something her mother had said didn't sit right with her.

"Why do you think Thomas Griffin will purchase you?" she asked. Then she shook her head with disgust, thinking about her mother being sold off like the family cow.

Hester patted her hand. "Mr. Griffin has always been kind to me, and his daughter needs a mother." She saw the skepticism in Abby's eyes, and added, "And there's more, child, though unseemly it would be to discuss the matter further."

Abby's eyes grew wide as saucers and she nearly voiced her

outrage. But then she thought of the man she'd met at the river crossing six months ago, and what happened during his last visit.

His name was Henry, and he'd come to her like a gift from above, on horseback, carrying a leather satchel filled with useful things. Fully grown, ten years older than she, Henry was a man of property, and close kin to Mayor Shrewsbury, the wealthiest, most powerful man in the colony, save for the governor himself. He was well-traveled and conversational, with an exhaustive inventory of colorful stories featuring far off lands and remarkable people.

Astonishingly, Henry had managed to show up three of the five times both her mother and stepfather happened to be gone. She now knew where her mother had been on those occasions, but how fortuitous for her that Henry always seemed to show up at the most opportune times.

She knew he was the man she'd marry, had known it from first sight. Not because he was tall and handsome, or rich and worldly, but because she could feel his presence from a great distance, even before he emerged from the woods. And not just the first time, but every time! If she could always feel his presence a quarter-hour before he arrived, how could this not be transcendent love? The powerful feeling he projected put her soul at ease, calmed her fears, and spoke to her heart.

Henry was coming.

She couldn't feel him yet, but he'd told her the day. He might miss the target by up to a week, for all plans were subject to weather, and he'd be traveling tricky terrain. But this time when he came to visit, she'd seal the deal. They'd ride off to town, get married, and she'd be free of this wretched life once and for all.

Abby was not ashamed that she'd given herself to Henry

during his third visit two months ago. Though he was twenty-seven years old, Henry was unmarried and available. She'd made him swear an oath to that effect before their first kiss. Though she hadn't expected to be taken so hastily her first time, much less from behind, Abby was pleased to know he shared her feelings of attraction. As for the event itself, she had known only the basics of what to expect, for her mother had spoken few words on the subject of fornication, and most of them only moments ago. But her Henry was obviously versed in the subject, so she put her trust in his expertise, and was at peace with her conscience.

Henry was coming for her. And soon.

Hester pushed a wisp of blonde hair from Abby's face and secured it behind her ear. The two women embraced again briefly, gave one last look around the clearing behind the slat-board shanty, and went inside the shack to start the dinner pot.

Inside, the heat was unbearable, and Abby's eyes took it all in: the dirt floor, the wormwood walls, the leaky roof, the rotten door. As she looked she was overcome with guilt over her mother's sacrifice. Hester had fended the man off as long as she could, and was willing to be humiliated and sold at public auction to give her daughter a chance at a decent life.

But while Abby loved the idea of killing Philip Winter, she had no intention of marrying and rutting the man in order to acquire his earthly possessions.

3.

CAPTAIN JACK HAWLEY held the spyglass to his eye and checked the shoreline surrounding Shark's Bay. He handed the glass back to his quartermaster, Pim, and took a moment to study the current. He knew what to expect, having made the Little River trip a dozen times before. It was a challenging bit of work, requiring hours of muscle-aching effort, but he was up to it. The idea of separating himself from the crew when they came to port was an extra precaution Jack had instituted upon being elected captain. More than one band of pirates had been ambushed and hung by soldiers working on orders from colonial governors, and Jack's subterfuge allowed him to infiltrate the settlement without creating undue suspicion, in order to ensure his crew would be able to land safely.

It probably wasn't necessary. Of all their shore stops, St. Alban's was the least dangerous. For one thing, there was no standing militia. For another, Jack's men were enthusiastically welcomed for the valuable supplies they generously shared with the town. On this particular weekend, while the crew planned to occupy themselves with drinking, gambling and whoring, Jack was looking forward to spending some quality time with the young girl he'd recently met.

The crew gathered around him on the open deck. No one spoke, though they were itching to hoist sail.

"I'll take Rugby," Jack said.

Pim shuffled his feet, ill at ease. "Rugby the cat, Sir?"

"You know any other Rugbys on board?"

Pim sighed. "It's a glad thing to wish for, but no, there be but one Rugby, as the devil himself can attest."

"Then that's the one I'll take."

Pim took a deep breath and looked the crew over to see if he could enlist some help. But most would rather jump off the side than go near the hairless, evil-looking cat.

"Mr. Pim," Jack said.

"Aye, Cap'n?"

"Are you still the roughest, toughest man aboard *The Fortress*?"

"To my knowledge I still be."

"And yet you're frightened at the prospect of getting a little pussy?"

The men sniggered.

"It ain't pussy in general that scares me, Cap'n, and my beloved Darla be proof of that fact. But this vile monstrosity and me don't get along so well."

"Then you'll be pleased to know this is her last voyage."

Then men punched each other's arms and spoke enthusiastically.

"Aye, Cap'n, that's good news indeed!" Pim said, smiling. He turned and made his way across the deck to the captain's quarters.

The symbiotic relationship between the town and pirates began years earlier when Milton Shrewsbury, Mayor of St. Alban's, made a deal with the privateer captains: if they agreed to police their crew and confine their shore activities to an area two miles from the town proper, he would construct a Free Zone at the North Port to include a general store, alehouse, gambling house, rooming house, and a house of prostitution. While in the Free Zone, the pirates could do as they wished, subject to captain's law. The town of St. Alban's benefited from the pirates' trade, of course, but also from the valuable gifts and sorely needed supplies the pirates freely donated.

"Come here, you fargin' banshee!" Pim shouted from within Jack's cubicle. The entire crew chuckled as Pim continued cursing Rugby. "Show yourself, you motherless cur! You evil vomitous bitch! Get out here, or I'll turn your hairless arse into a crossbones, you poisoned pig's pizzle!"

A pirate caught outside the Free Zone was subject to immediate imprisonment, a mandatory six-month sentence. If, in addition to being caught the pirate had committed a crime, the mayor could order him hung. By the same token, any St. Alban's woman found in the Free Zone, a.k.a. Sinner's Row, could not claim rape, should she be set upon by a drunken pirate or scallywag, subject to the pre-set rules of the ship's captain.

"Bull's blood!" shouted Martin, the boatswain, from the foredeck.

Jack looked in his direction. "Torn sail?"

"Aye," said Martin. "The jib."

"Satan's eye!" one of the men cursed. A torn jib sail could easily take an hour to repair.

"Set to it, then," Jack said, calmly.

Jack Hawley didn't look like the other pirates, even when dressed in full battle regalia. He was youthful in appearance, with fair skin and a smooth, unpoxed face that he kept clean-shaven. He had a full set of white teeth, and a well-muscled body.

"I'll head out now, and you can hoist anchor when she's repaired," Jack said.

Though an ambush was unlikely, Jack was cunning enough to want to keep his identity a secret. Indeed, last time in port, Mayor Shrewsbury had gone to the main pier of North Port with an entourage of businessmen to welcome the ship and asked for Hawley by name, and twenty men stepped forward claiming to be he.

Pim approached, having finally caught the cat-like animal. Rugby was unhappily bundled in a white silk scarf that featured French writing on all four borders. Pim pointed the surly beast's face away from him and held her tightly with both hands, as far away from his body as possible.

"The crew'll be breathin' a sigh of relief once you get this cursed creature off the ship," Pim said.

Captain Jack looked at the slender hairless cat and smiled. "I'm amazed the crew let her live this long."

"Only be due to your fondness for it, I'd wager."

Upon hearing Jack's voice, Rugby struggled to break free of Pim's giant hands. The savage hissing that escaped her mouth sounded more serpent than cat. Pim's eyes registered fright.

"May I set her down, Captain?"

Jack nodded, and Pim released his grip. Rugby, still tangled in the scarf, failed to make the proper adjustments for altitude and distance, and hit the floor hard. She shook the scarf off her body and offered a shrieking hiss that caused the quartermaster to shudder and grip the stock of his loaded pistol.

"She's unique, Pim."

"If I may say so, Cap'n, she's a monstrosity of nature who ain't right in the head. Some on board are convinced she's the devil's tit."

"And you, Mr. Pim?"

"I won't be goin' that far with my conjecturin', Cap'n, but I'm one a them that's gonna feel a hell of a lot safer when this malignant beast is mousin' on the mainland."

Jack laughed. "You should charge our musicians with composing a tune by that name."

Pim grinned. "Mousin'on the Mainland?"

"Aye. And you can pen the words."

"I'll do 'er," he said. Then added, "Provided you'll be pardonin' the language that might be defamin' Rugby's character."

"You're still upset over the beard incident."

Pim's eyes narrowed as he eyed the cat. Rugby caught the look and arched her back. "Hell of a way to be woke up, Cap'n. A man tries to catch a few winks and wakes to this hairless devil's spawn givin' 'im the evil eye, rippin' 'is chops, rakin' her claws over 'is face…"

"I can still hear your screams in my head."

"Aye, and I ain't the only one. That hairless bat ain't popular among them that's been woke similar in the crew."

Jack clucked softly, and Rugby turned to face him. She rubbed her body against his leg and purred. Jack dropped to one knee and scratched her ears. When he stopped, the ugly gray creature hopped effortlessly onto his shoulder. Jack stood and walked to the small dory and climbed in.

"You got your kit?" Pim said.

Jack reached under the front bench and removed the large leather satchel. He checked the contents, nodded, and strapped it over his shoulder. Pim signaled his team to lower the dory into the bay. The water foamed around the small wooden boat, causing Rugby to dig her claws into Jack's shoulder. Jack carefully extricated the cat and placed her on the floor of the boat. Rugby remained there until the first whitecap sloshed over the side, drenching her paws. Wanting no more of that, she jumped onto the front bench and pressed her body flat against it, locked her paws on either side, and held on for dear life.

Jack removed the hoist, secured his oars in the oarlocks, and began rowing toward shore. Over the next twenty minutes he worked the oars expertly, knifing the dory through the bay, while accepting minimal water from the heavy chop. Finally he steered his little boat into the still, sulfurous water of the Little River. He lifted an oar high above his head and waved it to let the crew know he was safe. Then he continued upriver.

The first bend was no more than fifty yards from the bay, but the high dunes and scrub brush effectively blocked the wind and made for stale air and stifling rowing conditions. Within minutes Jack was at his canteen, wiping his brow.

"That wasn't so bad, was it?" Jack said to his hairless companion.

Rugby didn't answer. She wasn't interested in conversation. Something had drawn her to the side of the boat, and she leaned out and over it, transfixed by something just below the waterline.

"I wouldn't put my face that close to the water," Jack warned. "If that's a snapping turtle you're tracking, it's apt to take your head off."

Rugby arched her back and hissed loudly, causing Jack to follow her gaze. He leaned over the side and shielded his eyes against the sun's glare on the water.

"What do you see down there that you haven't seen a hundred times, girl?"

In this part of the river the water was brackish, with light-green patches of algae hugging the shorelines. Whatever it was that had riled the cat was still troubling her, but Jack couldn't make it out.

Until he could.

"God's blood!" he exclaimed, jumping back in shock. There, just below the stagnant surface, he'd seen the hideous, human-like face of a yellow eel. Five feet long if an inch, and covered with dark brown spots that looked like eyeballs. Jack had never seen an eel in these waters before, let alone the eyeball markings. This one had obviously slithered out of one of the numerous limestone caves that lay beneath the waters of the Little River. A terrifying sight; and Jack shuddered to contemplate what manner of soulless, unknown species might be too large to escape the dark caves below his boat.

For the better part of an hour, into late afternoon, he navigated the river, relying on his sharp vision and keen intuition to evade the submerged tree limbs and sandbars that discouraged less skilled travelers from duplicating the journey. He and Rugby passed snakes, turtles, raccoons, skunks, cranes, and lily pads teeming with great, bellowing bullfrogs, and giant spiders mending their webs. Other than the occasional puff of hot breeze, the air was rank and stagnant, and filled with the odor of rotten eggs. Rugby winced and sneezed.

Jack laughed. "I know, smells like hellfire, don't it, girl? But it's just the sulfur pits that line these coves. We'll move past them soon."

He kept to the center of the river to avoid the thick, green pond scum that had all but taken over the river at this point, and the ravenous mosquitoes that hugged the verdant shore.

Rugby's ears pricked as they neared the final bend that led to their destination. Jack knew what his companion had heard. A moment later, he heard it too.

Children's voices.

Though he knew whose children they were, he stopped rowing, and kept his oars in the water to hold the boat in check. He listened a moment, studying the cadence of the voices. They sounded enthusiastic.

"Rugby, make nice, for they've assembled a landing party to greet us."

The cat looked at him and Jack said, "I don't know how they knew I was coming. But they always know. It's probably Rose, the witchy one. She senses things."

4.

THE LANDING PARTY, Jack knew, would number six: George and Marie Stout, their three young children, and Johanna, the young girl who lived and worked with the Stouts. Jack let out his signature whistle before rounding the final bend, and the voices immediately stopped, their minds processing the sound. Then, almost instantly, they began cheering. Jack had taught Johanna and the Stouts this particular whistle as a means of identifying themselves from a distance. He had taught them a danger whistle as well.

The group had gathered at the Stouts' dock, thirty yards west of George and Marie's outpost. For years the dock had been the primary means of accessing the outpost by the river families that settled on the banks north of this location. But the previous year's hurricane had deposited so many trees that the river north had become virtually impassable. These days, those who visited the outpost were forced to walk or ride the rough trail on horseback. Though the post was isolated, people willingly made the trip to obtain the one thing George had that they couldn't get elsewhere.

Medicine.

Medicine, the most prized and valuable commodity in the colonies, had been the foundation for Jack and George's close friendship. Other than gold, Jack's principal reason for attacking ships was to acquire medicine, which he sold and traded for goods and services. He had two paying customers in St. Alban's: the mayor's physician and Thomas Griffin, who owned the local apothecary. He also traded medicine with George Stout in return for information regarding the town's current attitude toward pirates, the unlimited use of George's horses, and care for Johanna, whom Jack had rescued from an abusive family two months earlier.

When the greeters saw Jack making the final turn, they cheered. But when they saw Rugby, George and Marie crossed themselves and spat over their shoulders. Even the children, accustomed to all manner of woodland creatures, crossed and spat, and hesitated to approach the boat.

Johanna was the lone exception. She sported a smile that seemed to occupy her entire face. When she bent down to accept the bow of the boat, she and Rugby eyed each other closely. Jack said, "This is Rugby. She's yours, if you want her."

Johanna squealed with joy, which caused Rugby to arch her back and hiss. One of the Stout boys yelped at the sound, and Marie recoiled in horror. But undaunted, Johanna put her hand out, and waited for Rugby to respond. Eventually the cat bent her head against Johanna's hand without launching an attack.

"She likes you," Jack said.

Looking pleased, Johanna steadied the boat and Jack climbed out. Giving the cat a wide berth, the Stouts gathered around Jack. Marie hugged him vigorously, and George clapped him on the back.

"Good to see you, Henry," he said, for that's the name Captain Jack used among the locals.

"Aye, and you and your family as well," Jack said. He looked at Johanna and nodded. "And you, miss. How are you?"

Johanna had picked Rugby up and cuddled her. Upon being addressed by Jack, she blushed and curtsied slightly. "The Stout family has taken excellent care of me, sir, and Mrs. Stout has been learning me to cook and clean."

"Such are good skills to have," Jack said, approvingly. He and Johanna looked at each other a moment, as if unsure what more to say. By contrast, the children were full of questions, most of which involved the cat.

Seven-year-old Samuel said, "Why do you call him Rugby?"

"She's named after her former owner, Colonel Rugby, of Glenshire."

"And what became of the Colonel?" the ultra-precocious, ten-year-old Rose asked. "Was it ghastly?"

"Rose, hush!" her mother scolded. "If Henry wants us to know what became of Colonel Rugby, it's for him to say, and not for us to ask."

Rose pointed a finger at the cat. "No matter," she said. "I suspect we'll all be dead by morning." Of all the Stout children, Rose was the least inclined toward optimism.

"Mind your tongue, child, or I'll cuff your ears!" Marie said, though Rose looked as though she might welcome such a cuffing. She was, in all respects, an unusual child, and her siblings weren't the only ones who regarded her as such. George and Marie learned early on to distance Rose from other families, after hearing visitors question whether she might be a witch.

Rose was not one of the Stout's birth children. According to George, he and Marie had found her four years earlier, wandering the woods, speaking in tongues. They took her in as they would any stray. From her first days with the Stouts, Rose had shown a particular fondness for heights and could routinely be found high in the branches of trees. According to

Samuel, Rose could talk to spiders, rats and snakes. Jack, though far less superstitious than most, always gave Rose a wide berth.

Jack watched Samuel tie his boat to the pier before speaking. "Colonel Rugby was set upon by either the French or pirates. I came upon their smoldering ship quite by accident, while fishing."

He and George exchanged a look as Jack continued his story. "When I boarded, I found not a single person or thing on it, apart from this strange cat-like creature. I did manage to salvage a portion of the captain's journal and read mention of Colonel Rugby's strange, furless cat. Not knowing the cat's original name, I named her for her former owner, and she seems to have accepted it without protest."

To Johanna he said, "Of course, she's yours now, miss, and you may change her name as suits you."

Rose said, "We could call her Calamity!"

"Calamity the Cat?" Samuel said. "That's obscene!"

"She's nakey!" said four-year-old Steffan.

George Stout said, "She does appear to be naked, compared to other cats I've seen."

Marie scolded her husband. "George, the children are present!"

George nodded and said, "Odd-looking animal, none-theless." He paused a moment. If he knew of any news Jack should worry about, he'd have told it by now. Instead, he clapped his hands and said, "Let's head to the house, Henry. I've a bottle of rotgut that's still got some kick left in it."

After carefully depositing Rugby on the dock, Johanna sidled up to Jack. It was clear from her body language and attentiveness that she found Jack not only attractive, but also desirable. While he understood it was the way of young women to want to marry and raise children, he loved his carefree life and preferred not to settle down in the near future. Had he met Johanna earlier, who knows what might have transpired? After all, she was sweet and charming, could hunt, fish, cook and sew, could skin animals and take care of children, was eager to work, was strong, and pleasing to the eye in all respects. In short, she possessed all the qualities that would make any man happy. But Jack resolved not to take advantage of Johanna, or lead her on, since he had another young lady in his sights, a girl named Abby Winter, whose mother had a gray face. Jack planned to ride to the river crossing to meet Abby early the next morning, and, if it pleased her, he intended to give her a good fucking.

Johanna leaned into Jack and rubbed the side of her face against his chest. He gave her a light, uncomfortable hug for her trouble, and they began walking toward the outpost.

Samuel worked up his courage and leaned over to pet the cat. "Does she bite?"

"She does," Jack said. "Fiercely."

Samuel paused with his hand a foot from the cat. "You think she'll bite me?"

"I'm certain of it."

"Even if I'm really nice and gentle?"

"Even if. She's quite independent, having survived a ship fire and starvation. Not many can claim that. After I rescued her she coughed up bits of rope and pitch, to show me what she'd eaten to survive."

"Devils eat pitch," said Rose. "They thrive in fiery places, too."

George said, "Rose, you're beginning to alarm us. Henry wouldn't bring a demon into our midst, would you Henry?"

"She's a sweet cat," Jack said. "A biter? Absolutely. But not a demon."

"There you have it," said Marie. "Now let's hear no more talk of devils and demons."

As they headed down the dock toward the outpost, Jack said, "How'd you know I was coming?"

They all looked at each other in a funny way, but no one spoke on it.

5.

THE CAT—OR whatever it was—adapted to its new surroundings quickly, and it dawned on Jack that perhaps cats had a natural preference for solid ground, and maybe this had contributed to Rugby's churlish behavior on board *The Fortress*. She moved gracefully around the yard surrounding the outpost, or "Stoutpost," as Jack liked to call it.

"What's become of your dogs?" he said.

"Lost one to a gator, we think. Sold the other one," George said.

"That works to Rugby's advantage."

"Till we get the next one, anyway. They wander in here regular, half-mad from hunger."

Jack smiled at Johanna.

"Rugby'll be fine. She can hold her own."

Johanna returned the smile.

George and Marie's tiny house and store were the southernmost dwellings on St. Alban's peninsula, a land mass of roughly thirty-six square miles, bordered, in part, by the Little River.

The men sipped their whisky at the table and watched Marie and Johanna tend the dinner pot. Rose had wandered off somewhere, and Samuel and Steffan were sharpening dinner knives.

"How's she fitting in?" Jack said.

"Johanna? She's a blessing."

"Any problems with her father?"

"Haven't seen him nor the wife since you threatened to kill them if they ever came back."

"That's good. I meant it. There's no excuse for a man to beat his children."

Jack stared at Johanna, thinking about the type of woman she'd grow up to be. She was too young for Jack, at least in his mind, but in a few years she'd be an ideal wife, devoted and grateful to him, and would probably be a wonderful mother to a brood of children as well.

George had noticed him staring at Johanna. He said, "I've only got the one bedroom."

Jack nodded. "That'll do."

George arched an eyebrow but said nothing.

Johanna, whose hearing was excellent, smiled at the comment, but didn't trust herself to peek at Jack. She was a thin, fair-skinned girl who'd come a long way from the waif he'd met two months earlier. Johanna had filled out some, thank the good Lord, and her face had gained color. She was a fine specimen, Jack thought, with her fair, unblemished skin, large green eyes and wavy saddle-brown hair made lighter by the scorching sun. The work dress she wore every day was gray and made of stout, twilled cotton that seemed too coarse for her delicate features. She had an easy smile and calm disposition, which was hard to fathom, given her past history of physical abuse by her parents. He'd been many places, seen many things, but not so many domestic scenes or settings. It was nice to see this healthy family working together to get food on the table.

In Jack's experience, American-born men and women were more pleasing to the eye and healthier than their European counterparts. Jack had twice been to London and seen the horrible living conditions. Everything about the city had the foulest stench. The people were permanently filthy, as no one took baths, including the wealthy. Poor families stitched their children into burlap clothes to be worn day and night through the entire winter. The houses, pinched together side by side in endless lines, cramped up against the edges of streets and roads, and men urinated freely onto the streets from second-floor windows. Avoiding the random soakings required careful planning. One couldn't just move to the center of the street, for that's where the latrines had been dug. Women pitched the contents of their chamber pots into the streets daily, without offering the slightest pretense of embarrassment. The refuse and human excrement would be scattered across the dirt or cobblestones awaiting the next rain to wash it into the latrine. Therefore, at any given time, the streets were cesspools so filled with urine and horse manure that no one bothered to avoid stepping in it. Worse, it soaked and clung to the hems of the long dresses and coats worn by women, to be slathered throughout their homes and the commercial establishments they frequented.

If the living conditions were bad, the faces were worse.

Ninety percent of the population had suffered from smallpox or chickenpox at one time or other, and their faces and bodies were riddled with deep-pocketed scars. Rashes, funguses and open sores could be found on nearly every face, at any time. By age twelve, most had rotting teeth. Those who managed to live past the age of thirty did so without their teeth. Infection and oozing pus adorned the vast majority of necks, backs and buttocks; and boils and carbuncles were constant sources of annoyance and pain.

Of course, the major cities in America were filthy, but

towns such as St. Alban's, while nasty in certain areas, benefited from the lack of dense population. Though George and Marie's faces were pockmarked and their teeth bad, they still managed to look ten years younger than their European counterparts. And thanks to the rural living conditions, healthy food, and medicine supplied by their good friend Jack, Johanna and the Stout children appeared healthy and clear-skinned enough to be a different species altogether.

"See any pirates when you were fishing?" Samuel said.

"Not this trip."

"We like pirates, don't we, Father?" Rose said.

George and Marie exchanged a glance. They knew Jack was a pirate, but it wouldn't be safe for their children to know.

Jack said, "I think all colonists are fond of pirates, or privateers, as they're currently called. Reason being, English taxes are so high these days, the colonists lose money on every crop. They have to traffic with pirates to survive."

"Do you know any pirates, Henry?" Rose said.

Jack could feel all eyes on his face. "It's possible, since there are pirates everywhere these days."

"How come?" Samuel persisted.

"With England at war with Spain, they want pirates to sink Spanish ships. So they passed a law that lets pirates keep 100 percent of their plunder from enemy ships."

"England *likes* pirates?" Samuel asked.

Jack laughed. "England tolerates them for now. But when the war is over, that will change."

"What will happen then?"

"The governors will go back to hanging them."

6.

THE OUTPOST WAS connected to the main house by a heavy wooden door with iron banding. The main room contained a couple dozen shirts and pants, assorted ropes, netting, hammers, saws, nails and other hardware, much of which had been previously used. The medicine and knives weren't kept in this building, but in locked trunks in George's bedroom. Behind the service counter, another door led to a small bedroom that George and Marie rented to customers by the night. Those who slept here were usually too sick to travel, so it was more of a treatment room than a hotel.

After supper, while the men talked at the main table, Marie and Johanna put some linens and a blanket on the guest bed and set out a clean chamber pot. Rose fetched some well water for the basin, and Johanna placed a towel and hand mirror beside it.

"Do you have any questions about what might happen tonight?" Marie said.

Johanna blushed.

"I know you've probably seen it done, but this will be different."

Johanna looked down at her hands in her lap.

Marie said, "Well then, I'll just let nature take its course. Tomorrow, if you want, we can talk about what happened.

"Okay."

Marie walked to the doorway, turned, and smiled. Johanna said, "Don't worry, Mrs. Stout. Everything will be all right."

Marie looked at the young girl sitting on the bed, her work dress caked with grime from the day's cleaning. Johanna's hair was a tangled mess, and soot smudges from the firewood covered her hands and right forearm. There were random smudges on her forehead where she'd wiped her brow. Her legs and ankles were bruised and cut from the brambles and saw grass, and there were chigger bites on her cheek and neck.

It was a pitiful sight to behold.

Marie sighed. "Here, child, let me work on you a bit."

She dipped the towel in the water basin and scrubbed Johanna's face, neck, and arms, then rinsed it off.

She stepped back to survey her work, frowned and shook her head.

"Take your shoes off."

Marie scrubbed the girl's feet, rinsed the towel again and handed it to her, saying, "I'll leave the room a moment while you clean the rest of you."

Marie closed the door behind her and went to one of the cabinets in the store. George and Marie didn't stock luxury items like dresses, but they did have a couple of nightshirts. Marie chose one, shook it out, and put it to her nose. It smelled slightly of mildew, but was a vast improvement over Johanna's shift. She waited a couple minutes and knocked on the door. When Marie entered the bedroom holding the nightshirt, Johanna jumped to her feet and hugged her tightly.

"I love you, Marie," she said.

Marie smiled and patted her back. "Well, it's the least I can do."

After Marie left, Johanna changed clothes and sat on the side of the bed to wait for Henry. A moment passed and she heard the slightest movement under the bed. She jumped to her feet. Her eyes darted around the room searching for any type of weapon she could use to kill a snake or rat, but found nothing. Fine, she'd use her shoe if she had to. Johanna grabbed a shoe, set her jaw, knelt beside the bed, lifted the low-hanging edge of the quilt and carefully looked beneath it.

She gasped and drew back.

It wasn't a snake or rat.

It was Rose.

Johanna grabbed her by the foot and pulled her out.

"You monstrous child!" she said. "What were you doing under there?"

"Why, waiting for you and Henry to fornicate, of course."

7.

THE FORTRESS HAD been anchored a hundred yards offshore for nearly two hours and the men were getting surly. Those who owned spyglasses had climbed high up the netting to focus them—not on the south side of St. Alban's, where smoke would be visible had the captain uncovered a plot to capture them—but on the docks of Sinner's Row, where the whores were hooting and hollering and showing off their wares. The spotters were whipping the crew into a frenzy with their running commentary.

Pim frowned. The captain specifically said to wait four hours for a signal. On the other hand, *The Fortress* had torn a sail back in Shark's Bay and that had set them back nearly an hour while they waited for Martin to repair it. So technically they *had* waited nearly three hours since lowering the captain's dory.

"C'mon, Pim," Roberts said. "If there was a fire, I'd have seen it by now! Give the order, and let's go ashore!"

Pim had full authority to act in the captain's absence. Like the captain, a pirate ship's quartermaster was an elected position, worth an extra share of the booty. Pim's job was to represent the interests of the crew, settle their differences, and maintain order. He also distributed food and medicine, and divided up the booty. Pim was as eager to go ashore as any man on board, since he intended this to be his final shore leave, should Darla agree to give up whoring, settle down and marry him. He had reason to believe she might. They'd grown close over the years, and he regretted not asking her two months ago like he'd planned. He called to Roberts in the crow's nest. "Give 'er one last, careful sweep with the scope. If she's clean, we'll put the first boat ashore and watch what happens. If that goes well, we'll move in another fifty, aim her sideways to the port to show her guns, and go ashore, 'cept for the skeleton crew."

One long minute later a cheer rang out among the crew when Roberts confirmed the absence of smoke. An hour after that, Pim and the last landing party were standing on the pier at Sinner's Row. By then, all the prostitutes were occupied, so Pim and the others split up into smaller groups of gamblers, drinkers and shoppers. Pim made his way to the Blue Lagoon, entered, and took his usual seat in the far corner. He looked around the place with anxious eyes.

Pirates weren't allowed to drink before battles or while under sail. Nor were they allowed to drink to excess at any time while on the vessel, and Pim was no exception. But on shore, he was an accomplished drinker with a particular fondness for Puerto Rican rum and a thick-waisted whore named Darla. After four years of shore excursions it was common knowledge that Darla and Pim were a couple when he was in town. Though pirates in general were a hard lot, only the drunkest of the tough would think to challenge Pim on this or any other issue, since Pim was known to have a long memory and it fell to him to discipline the crew at sea. An affront on shore could mean the difference between being lashed or keelhauled at sea, and, though neither was pleasant, on a ship as large as *The Fortress*, keelhauling was often a death sentence.

The way it worked, the victim was tied to two ropes that were looped beneath the ship. One was tied to his wrists, the other around his ankles. Then he was thrown overboard, and dragged under the keel and up the other side of the ship. Since the keel was encrusted with sharp barnacles, sheets of his skin would be scraped off in salt water, which is even more painful than it sounds. Some who lived were subjected to a second trip, if their infraction warranted it.

The Blue Lagoon was owned and operated by a large, nervous man known as One-Eyed Charlie Fine, who got his name after betting one of his eyes on a ten-high straight in a poker game with a pirate named Ginhouse Jim. Jim had a full house, sixes over one-eyed jacks.

Charlie owned a piece of the unnamed whorehouse next door to the Blue Lagoon. As the primary beneficiary of Pim's inebriated generosity, Charlie had learned long ago that it made good business sense to pull Darla from the line-up when *The Fortress* was in town, to waitress Mr. Pim till closing. As this had become a time-honored tradition, Pim was surprised to see a different waitress standing before him.

"Darla's gone," she said.

"Gone? What d'you mean, gone? Gone where?"

"She died. Want a drink?"

Pim blinked a couple of times and shook his head as if to help her words make sense.

"You mean to tell me Darla's dead?"

"Dead as a brick, yes, sir."

Pim tilted his head, as if the world were somehow askew, and this would help him see it better. He cleared his throat and swallowed. It didn't make sense. Two months ago she'd been radiant, full of life. He forced his voice to work.

"What happened?"

196

"Cramp colic."

So out of the blue her appendix had burst and killed her and he'd had no chance to say goodbye. Pim had always assumed that one day he'd give up piracy and make an honest woman of her. And now…

"Sir?"

He looked at her.

"I know Darla's gone, but I can take her place."

Pim's mind seemed to be floating away. He could barely make out her words.

"Take her place?"

"I can serve you till you've had your fill, then, if you want, I'll go with you upstairs like Darla used to."

Pim tried to comprehend the magnitude of his loss. Darla, the only woman on earth who cared what happened to him. He briefly tried to contemplate a life without Darla in it. But the woman standing in front of him had said something he didn't quite catch. He tried to focus.

"I'm sorry," Pim said. "You're what?"

"A good whore, sir."

"Oh."

"Mr. Fine picked me personal, 'cause I get no complaints. And if it suits you, I'll stay all night in your bed, just like Darla did."

Pim stared at nothing awhile longer before finally letting out a huge, mournful sigh. Then he said, "What's your name?"

"Grace, sir."

"Did you know Darla?"

"Know her?"

"I mean, were you friends?"

She looked confused by the question.

"We don't get much opportunity to have friends here, sir.

And there's some competition for the half-sovereigns and up. But Darla, well, she was pleasant, never stole nothing I know about."

Pim nodded slowly.

"Grace?"

"Yes, sir?"

"Yellow rum."

"Okay."

"And lots of it."

"Thank you, sir."

8.

TWO HOURS OF drinking had done nothing to diminish Pim's sorrow. He waved off Grace's offer to sit with him while he drank, and Charlie Fine stopped by the table to offer his condolences. But in the end Pim put his hands over his eyes, bent his head to the table and cried like a baby. When Martin and Roberts entered the bar and saw their enormous friend sobbing fit to bust they fled the premises as if frightened by fairies. Charlie Fine told Grace to get Pim upstairs before he chased off the rest of the customers.

Grace reluctantly approached the red-haired giant and patted his back. She pushed one side of her blouse down her shoulder and revealed a breast of adequate size and smoothness, which she rubbed against the side of Pim's impossibly hairy face. He lifted his head and she moved her breast to his lips.

"Come upstairs with me now, sir," she said, softly.

Pim's lower lip quivered. He seemed about to burst into tears again, but at the last minute he pushed his chair back and got to his feet. Grace quickly tucked her bosom back into her blouse and took Pim's hand and led him up the steps.

The room upstairs had belonged to Darla when Pim was in town, and everything about it reminded him of her. Though Grace shucked her clothes off in record time, and despite the fact that most men would consider her body vastly superior to Darla's, Pim was having none of it.

"If you'll allow me, I'll undress you now, sir."

"I can't. I'm sorry."

"Please, sir."

"Why do you give a shit?"

"He'll beat me if you leave here unsatisfied."

Pim frowned and shook his head. It was a bad life. Bad for Grace, and bad for Darla before her. He wondered if Charlie Fine had beaten Darla. If he knew for sure he'd kill Charlie with his bare hands. But he didn't want to know. It didn't matter now anyway. He stuffed his big paw into his pocket and felt around till he found a sovereign and a five guinea. He handed them to the naked woman in front of him and watched her eyes widen.

"The sovereign's for Charlie Fine. You keep the five guinea."

"Are you sure, sir?"

He pressed her fingers over the gold coin and kissed them.

"Maybe next time," he said.

Grace's eyes welled with tears. She stood on tiptoes to reach his cheek. Kissed him and said, "You were special to her. I think she may have loved you."

Pim smiled for the first time since hearing the news of Darla's death. It was a sad smile just the same.

"I'll never forget her," he said.

Now, standing on the dirt road in front of the Blue Lagoon, Pim tried to decide what he wanted to do. Had it been a matter of what to do for the night, he would have climbed into one of the dories, slept it off and caught a ride back to the ship come morning. But this was a question of what to do with the rest of his life, and for that he needed a sign.

On the pier, in the distance, two of his men were cursing

blue blazes and trying to fight a drunken duel using the crudest of implements. The one-armed man wielding the three-legged stool seemed to have an advantage over the one-legged guy with the chicken, but it was hard to imagine them doing much damage to each other. The stool was too heavy for the one guy to swing, and the live chicken was giving the other one fits. Pim had to admire their determination, but wondered what it said about the quality of life he was living.

If only God would send him a sign.

He walked a few minutes, then stopped and looked around. The night air was hot and thick with mosquitoes and fat, buzzing June bugs. Bats and barn swallows darted about with wild abandon, coming from all angles to feast on the bug buffet.

Pim wondered if perhaps the sign was something to be heard instead of seen. He turned his body slowly, making a complete circle, listening intently. But all he heard were peals of drunken laughter, assorted curses and squawks from the ongoing pier battle, and the occasional shriek of whores feigning orgasm.

Any kind of sign would suffice.

He waited a moment longer and then started walking aimlessly down the road.

Toward St. Alban's.

And just like that, the course of history was about to change.

9.

CAPTAIN JACK HAWLEY bade George Stout goodnight and knocked at the door to the room where Johanna sat waiting. Moments earlier he'd been shocked to see George's ghoulish daughter, Rose, hanging by her heels from a rope in the center of the store.

He rushed toward her.

"Are you all right? Who did this to you?" he said.

As he drew near, she opened her eyes and made a terrifying face at him.

Jack said, "Fine. Get yourself down."

Rose laughed and pulled herself up the rope, all the way to the beam. Jack marveled at her dexterity. Once atop the beam, she began untying her ankles. Jack turned away and started walking toward the bedroom where Johanna was waiting.

Rose shouted "Catch me!"

Jack turned and was horrified to see Rose plummeting toward the floor. He dove under her and caught her just before impact.

She got to her feet, clapped the dust off her hands and said, "Why, thank you, Henry!" and headed off to bed.

Jack gathered himself to a standing position and let out a deep breath. Though not a religious man, he made the sign of the cross on his chest. When Johanna opened the door, he said, "If you like Rugby's looks, you'd best keep her away from Rose. She's apt to cast a spell to cover Rugby's body with feathers."

Johanna giggled. She took Jack's hand, kissed it and pressed it to her bosom vigorously, in a way that revealed the entire contents of her nightshirt to his touch. Jack jerked his hand away as if he'd touched a hot stone. His face contorted into a horrified expression.

"Please don't be angry," she said. "I know I'm small, but that will change ere long."

"But...But you're—" Jack sputtered, unable to form a sentence.

Johanna smiled. "I'm ready, Henry. It's our time. I'm not experienced, but you'll teach me."

"I'll do nothing of the sort," he said with a huff.

He led her to the bed and sat her down. She, on the verge of tears, said "Why not?"

"You're...for God's sake, you're...you're only twelve years old!"

Johanna stuck her chin out in defiance.

"And so what if I am? My mother was twelve when she married, and her mother, too. And Marie as well. And all of them pregnant before turning thirteen!"

"It's obscene."

"It's life, Henry."

"It's wrong."

"How old was your mother when she had you?"

He waved his hand dismissively. "I don't know," he lied.

"Truly?"

Jack frowned. "It's not something I wish to think about in any case."

Johanna started crying. Softly at first, and then it began to build.

"You don't love me," she sobbed.

"I barely know you!"

"It *always* starts with barely knowing," she said, trying to catch her breath between sobs. "Then it grows. Ask anyone."

"You're a child," he said, instantly regretting the remark when he saw the heartbreak in her eyes. A few seconds passed before she exploded into a frenzy of tears, and when it happened, Jack felt awful. But he was a practical man, and what he'd said couldn't be taken back, so he kissed her forehead and turned away. He walked to the foot of the bed and eased himself to the floor where soon he fell asleep, even as she cried her eyes out a few feet away on the bed.

Four hours later Jack began tossing and turning. He spoke in his sleep of a thin, blonde girl from long ago or far away who kept saying her name. Johanna wanted to wake him out of his dream, in case it was a nightmare, but she couldn't afford to make him angry again, not if she intended to get her family started.

And she did so intend.

But getting her family started, as everyone knew, began with the process of rutting.

On the subject of rutting, Johanna knew she had a lot to learn. That men wanted to rut was not a question. But perhaps not all men were like her father, who rutted at night in a violent, angry way after consuming serious quantities of liquor. Maybe her Henry was the type of man who preferred to rut in the morning.

Johanna yawned. She was exhausted from the long day's work, fatigued from crying half the night over Henry's rejection, and these were too many issues for her to ponder. Tomorrow would be another day, a better day, and maybe Henry would wake up refreshed and ready to rut. Johanna closed her eyes and settled into her pillow. She could wait until tomorrow to ask about his dream. Tomorrow morning, after rutting, she'd ask Henry who Libby Vail was.

At that very moment, four miles away in downtown St. Alban's, Pim finally got his sign.

It had taken him well over an hour to stumble the two miles of dark road from Sinner's Row to town, and once there he spied a lodging house a couple of blocks away. As he headed there to get a room he saw a crudely written bulletin nailed to a post. Pim wasn't an accomplished reader, but he'd learned enough of his letters to make out the gist of the announcement: the next morning at noon someone's wife was going to be auctioned off in the town square.

Auctioned off? Someone's wife?

Pim looked up and thanked God for sending such a bold sign. He meant to have a look at this woman, and if she pleased him, buy her.

10.

THE NEXT MORNING Jack was up and out the door before Johanna or any in the family had stirred. He saddled a horse and led it out of the pen. Then he heard a sound that made him look up and stop dead in his tracks: Rose was standing on the roof of the store, her hands stretched upward. He looked around the perimeter of the building but could see no ladder, barrel or box. The height was ten feet, maybe more.

"How'd you get up there?" he said.

"I flew."

"Then fly down. If you jump, I won't be here to catch you this time."

Jack climbed on his horse and barely cleared the yard before her laughter started. He dug his heels into the horse's ribs and bolted through the brush. So fierce was her laughter he could hear it half a mile away. Or maybe it was the earlier laughter still ringing in his ears.

"I'm glad *she's* not the one in love with me!" he said to his horse.

The river crossing was a mile and a half from George and Marie's, but the path to it was muddy and overgrown with thickets and scrub pines.

When Abby saw him she smiled.

Jack's face and neck had been sliced by foliage. His shoulders and sides ached from the pounding and thwacking of tree branches. He climbed off his horse feeling like he'd been in a bar fight, but a fight that he'd won.

With Abby Winter the prize.

"Each time I've come, you've been here waiting," he said.

"I always know when you're nearby," Abby said. "I can *feel* it."

They kissed. And kissed again and again, short, happy bursts that often missed the mark and made them laugh.

"Did you also know I was here?" she said.

"I hoped you would be, but had you not, I would have whistled."

"My father sleeps soundly, though my mother might have heard."

"It's best to keep our doings quiet," Jack said.

Abby put a finger to his lips. "No longer," she said.

"Excuse me?"

"Much has happened since last we met. And I have great good news!"

"You do?"

"Yes. I'm apt to burst from waiting to share it!"

"Then do so, please."

Abby took a deep breath. As she let it out her eyes danced. "We're getting married!"

Jack stood there, his smile frozen on his face.

"Who is?"

She looked at him like he had two heads. "Why, you and I, of course!"

Jack felt as though he'd been chucked in the head with a yardarm.

"What's wrong?" she said.

"Did you speak of marriage? You've caught me by surprise."

207

Abby smiled. "It's the perfect time. Nay, sir, it's the *only* time."

Jack cocked his head quizzically. "But how can this be the only time?"

"My mother's being sold today."

"She's...*what*?"

Abby sighed. "Being sold. Today."

"Sold? You don't mean sold. What's the word you're seeking?"

"The only word I'm seeking is the one I used. She's to be sold in the town square at noon today, and that's a fine fact."

"Do you mean to say you can actually sell your wife to another man in these Florida colonies?"

"Well, of course you can! Where have you been?"

"And you don't need her permission?"

"Well, of course you need her permission! How can you not know these things? Are you not related to Mayor Shrewsbury?"

Jack paused. "In a roundabout manner of speaking, yes."

"Well the connection wasn't so 'roundabout' the last time we met, was it?"

"The connection to Mayor Shrewsbury is a bit fuzzy, but there is one. In general."

"Then you should know about these things. How can you not?"

"These ideas regarding the selling of wives never came up."

"Perhaps they did and you forgot."

Jack doubted that.

"So," he said. "How much will she fetch?"

"What?" She slapped his face. "Why? Do you mean to marry me, plow me like a field and sell me to some degenerate scallywag?"

"Why, no!"

"Well then, we need to move this thing along. I've been waiting day and night for your return, with no means of contacting you to tell you my news."

"About your mother being sold?"

"No, you nit! About this!" She pulled her nightshirt high enough to accommodate his hand, and helped him feel her belly. Before he could recoil in horror, she lifted his hand higher, and pressed it to her swollen breasts. What was it about these St. Alban's women? Last night Johanna, now Abby. To Jack it seemed to be raining titties! He'd never felt so many breasts in such a short period of time. Of course, while Abby Winter's breasts were only three years older than Johanna's, there was clearly a difference to the touch, and it was this difference that stirred something in Jack.

Which is how she got the swelling in the first place.

Abby looked radiant, and Jack's heat was all-consuming. "Can we…?"

She looked around. "Not here. Walk with me a bit."

"But I…"

"Walk with me. It's not far."

Jack forced his thoughts elsewhere as they walked toward the brush on the far side of the crossing.

"What about your father?" he said, searching for a way to extricate himself from the possibility of marriage. "Surely we'd need his blessing?"

"He's not my father, he's my stepfather and he means to marry me the moment he's sold my mum. Then I'll be slaving for this pig of a man even as he ruts and beats me half to death."

"He can't be that bad."

"He can and he is. Wait—why would you say that? Do you

209

mean to abandon me to my stepfather after troubling yourself
to bend me over last time and seed me with child?"

"The way you're putting that…"

"Yes?"

"I mean, it weren't no trouble to do it, it was a pleasure!"

"Well, how nice! I'm so glad to hear how much pleasure
you took in deflowering me. And now that you've had your
pleasure, where does this put us, sir?"

Jack didn't know, but he figured she'd correct him if he
said the wrong thing.

"We should definitely be together, I suppose."

"Well there's a start," Abby said. Then, "Do you mean to
say you've never given this a thought prior to now?"

"I guess it never came up in my thoughts."

"The selling of wives never came up. Marrying the girl you
impregnated never came up. I'll suggest in your world the
only thing that comes up is your prick, sir."

Jack didn't know what to say. Up to now, his experience
with women had been confined to whores and platonic
friendships. Well, there had been a brief fling with a female
pirate a few years back, but that encounter served to hurt his
dignity more than it offered insight into the workings of a
proper woman's mind. Jack didn't remember much of what
happened that night in Tortola with the female pirate, except
that she'd been rough enough to blush a whore. Now, years
later, people still told the tale of Jack Hawley and Dorothy
Spider's sexual congress. There was even a popular song
composed to commemorate the occasion, which is why to this
day Jack refused to dock in Tortola.

"Henry?"

Dorothy had been a savage pirate and fierce bar brawler
whose face bore the marks of many battles. While not pirating,

she lived in Tortola with a famously fat female tattoo artist named Helen, who lovingly covered Dorothy's battle scars with tattoos. By the time she finished, Dorothy's face looked so much like a spider web that Helen decided to continue etching, to complete the theme. It was right around that time that Dorothy Spider caught Jack in her web during a misguided moment of high heat and heavy drink on his part, and the rest, as they say, is legend.

"*Henry*," Abby persisted. "Whatever is on your mind? Do you not see me lying on the ground with my legs bent? Is this not why we came to the bushes? So you could spread a little more seed while considering whether or not to abandon me? Perhaps you can thrust hard enough to give me twin bastards to rear on my own. Oh, please do! It will be fun to have this lovely memory in my head in the years to come when my stepfather violates my body and pounds my eyes with his fists."

This visit wasn't turning out quite the way Jack had envisioned during the ride over. The beautiful, shy, and charming Abby Winter had somehow turned into what Pim and his mates would at best call a saucy wench. But he had to admit, the view she currently afforded him was an outstanding one, and if Abby meant to give him a ride while angry, maybe she'd give him even better rides in the future if he could find a way to keep her happy.

And so it was with these thoughts that he smiled and dug in and tried not to think of Dorothy Spider.

11.

PIM WOKE TO the chatter in the street. He looked around and realized he'd failed to make it to the lodging house and had instead passed out in the street, where he'd thrown up at least once, and rolled around numerous times in raw sewage. He knew not what time it was, but the auction hadn't started yet, and he was eager to get a front-row seat. Checking his pockets and money pouch to make sure he hadn't been robbed, he mentally calculated the worth of a used wife and decided he had money to spare.

But wait—had he imagined it?

He got to his feet and went to the post where he'd seen the sign. In the light of day he had no problem reading the bulletin:

> NOTICE OF A WIFE TO BE SOLD AT NOON
> ST. ALBAN'S TOWN SQUARE
> SATURDAY, JULY 19, 1710
>
> IN ACCORDANCE WITH ENGLISH LAW THAT
> PROVIDETH A MAN MAY SELL HIS WIFE IF HE
> DO SO IN OPEN MARKET AND SHE GIVETH HER
> PERMISSION BY WEARING A HALTER ROUND
> HER NECK;
>
> THIS MAN, PHILIP WINTER, SHALL SELL HIS

**WIFE HESTER IN SUCH A MANNER ON
SATURDAY THE 19TH OF JULY, 1710.**

**BUYER MUST AGREE TO ACCEPT HESTER
WINTER AS SHE BE, WITH ALL HER FAULTS.**

Pim wanted to make himself more presentable by jumping in the river or ocean, whichever was closer, but after inquiring the time from a horrified passer-by, he was afraid he'd miss the auction. He went to the nearest house and knocked on the door and offered to pay a half-crown for a basin of water.

"That's a fair price for the basin," the woman allowed, "but where would I get another? You'll have to try someone else."

"I'd be buyin' only the water in the basin, Mum."

"What? Are you daft? Be gone, or I'll call my husband."

Pim produced the coin.

"I've only got used water," she said.

"How used?"

"Two days' worth. But it's a full basin. You want it?"

"Aye, and a rag to scrub with."

The lady of the house eyed Pim closely, scrunched her nose and said, "Is that vomit in your beard?"

"Aye, Mum."

"Well in that case you may keep the rag. I wouldn't want to touch it after you've used it."

"You're too kind."

"I'd rather bring a horse turd into my home."

"Yes, Mum. Thank you."

Pim did what he could with the basin of used water, though it smelled worse to him than he did. When he got to the town square he sat on a rock and waited for Captain Jack, who he sensed was drawing near. Ten minutes later Jack Hawley was standing over him, chewing him out.

"Are you insane? If they see you here they'll lock you up!"

"I'm not a pirate no more, Cap'n."

"What?"

"My sweet Darla's dead, and I'm gonna buy this wife what's bein' sold today."

This was shaping up to be Jack's most interesting shore leave ever. He tried to picture Abby Winter's mother marrying the wild and wooly pirate, Mr. Pim. An unintended smile crossed his face.

"What's so funny?" Pim growled.

"Easy, man. I'm sorry for your loss. I never met Darla, but I know she was special to you. I meant no offense by the smile. It's just the thought of you settling down. Pim: a landlubber!"

Pim nodded. Then said, "You know this woman what's to be sold today?"

"I don't, though I suspect she'll be happy to marry a kind-hearted soul such as yourself."

"Thank you, Jack. I'm not picky. I'm sure she'll do."

Jack looked him over. "You're sober?"

"Mostly. I think."

"Good. Looks like you had a rough night pining for Darla."

"Aye. And I drank some, too."

"And coughed some back, by the look of it."

"Aye."

"You need some money?"

"Why, thank you, Cap'n, but no, I did no whorin' so I'm flush."

"Well, do me a favor and act like you know me not."

A hurt expression creased Pim's face.

Jack said, "I'm not ashamed to be in your company, but if

some townie recognizes you, they'll lock us both up and I won't be able to rescue you."

Pim nodded. "Aye, you always was a smart one, Cap'n."

"And Mr. Pim?"

"Aye?"

"I'm proud to have served with you."

Pim's eyes moistened. "It's been an honor, Jack."

"Good luck, man."

"Thank you, sir."

12.

WIFE-SELLING ALWAYS followed the same public ritual. The wife—in this case, the gray-faced but comely Hester Winter—was led into town by her husband Philip with her hands bound and a halter around her neck. In most cases, wife-selling was a spur of the moment decision, and the husband had to make a big noise to draw a crowd. But the enterprising Philip had thought to post notice of his upcoming sale, and so the town square was packed with leering men, derisive women, and ill-mannered children, most of whom shouted profanities and vulgar insults at Hester.

As Philip got his wife onto the auction block, he displayed a wide, shit-eating grin and bade the crowd to gather near, since he was preparing to take bids. Hester's eyes searched the crowd, hoping to spot Thomas Griffin, but there were too many people. From behind her, a crude boy of about nine jumped onto the block and lifted the back of her skirt with one hand and held his nose with the other as his friends hooted and jeered. Philip laughed and swatted at the boy in a playful manner, which did nothing to dissuade him from raising Hester's dress again, and higher. Soon, half a dozen brats were taking turns spanking her rump Finally Philip called an end to the abuse.

"Who'll offer me a crown?"

"Does her privates work?" one man shouted.

Hester squeezed her eyes shut and reminded herself a better life was moments away.

"Her privates?" Philip said. "They work right well, mate, if your equipment be long enough to reach the prize." He gave an exaggerated stage wink and received some scattered chortling in return.

"Does she cook?" said another.

"She ain't the worst I've et," Philip said.

"How much discount are you offering for that face?" the fishmonger's wife yelled out.

"Already factored in the bidding, Missus. Why, are you interested in marryin' her yourself?" Philip made a lewd gesture and the crowd laughed.

Hester was thankful Philip had made Abby stay home. Thomas Griffin had obviously changed his mind, and now that she thought about it, why wouldn't he? He was a respectable businessman with a shop on the far side of the square. If he purchased her he'd be a laughing stock. Hester hadn't considered that possibility the three times she let him take her behind the counter. Ah well, men lied. What could she do about it now but accept her fate.

"I'll give the crown," someone said.

Hester opened her eyes and found the bidder, a young man, twenty at most, with curly brown hair and a lopsided grin that showed some gnarled brown teeth. Half his face was puckered from a fire, and he was missing an ear on that side. But he had broad shoulders and looked strong, and seemed kind.

Hester smiled at him.

"See that, son? She likes you!"

Someone else offered a sovereign, someone Hester couldn't see from her vantage point. She thought how strange it would be if she wound up married to someone she'd never even seen before.

"How 'bout it son?" Philip said to the curly-haired boy. "Can you beat a sovereign?"

Hester looked at him hopefully. He might not be much to look at, she thought, but she had facial problems of her own, and no right to complain. This boy wasn't a Thomas Griffin in appearance or property, but he seemed a step above her husband.

The boy looked at Hester with sorrow in his eyes. He mouthed the words, "I'm sorry," and she nodded.

"Don't that just break your heart folks?" Philip said. "Is there no one here who'll lend this poor boy a few paltry coins to help him find his true love?"

"Can we work it out in trade?" said a crippled man with a scar on his scalp that was so large and had healed so poorly, it looked like he'd grown a colony of little pink mushrooms on his head.

Hester shuddered.

"Don't think she likes you, Grady," Philip said.

The crowd was calm for a moment. Grady's head had that effect on people.

"How's her titties?" said a large man with a serious facial tick and a hole where his left eye should have been.

"Well if it ain't One-Eyed Charlie Fine!" Philip said. "What're you doin' in town when all them privateers be in port up yonder?"

"You'll know soon enough why I'm here and not there," Charlie Fine said. "But if this iron-headed bitch has titties to make up for that godawful face, she might be worth a piece of eight."

The crowd murmured with amazement. Pieces of eight

218

were Spanish silver coins of near-perfect purity. A piece of eight represented a month of work for a common man of the time.

Philip Winter was stunned by the price. "You figure to put her to work at the whorehouse?"

"I do, if an eight'll buy her and her tits be fair."

Philip Winter licked his lips and looked at his wife. Hester shook her head no. Philip, proving he knew how to work a crowd, said, "Who else here wants to see her tits?"

The crowd went wild and Philip approached his wife.

Before he got there, a shot rang out. Everyone froze for a split second, then ducked for cover. The man who'd shot his pistol into the dirt looked like a crazed drunk. His fiery red hair was matted with manure and he had enormous red mutton chops that were caked with dried vomit. When he spoke, his voice was gravely but firm.

Charlie Fine's face went white. He approached Pim and whispered, "What the hell're you doin' here?"

"Back off, Charlie," Pim said. "I ain't in the business no more, so I'm free to be here." To the auctioneer, Pim said, "I'll give you a solid-gold Spanish doubloon."

The crowd jumped to their feet as one, oohing and aahing. Hester searched Pim's face for guile and his eyes for sanity.

Philip Winter said, "That's very funny, Mister...what's your name?"

"My surname's Pim, and that's how I'm called. I'll buy this beautiful woman and treat her like the lady I know she be."

"Well now, no offense intended, Pim, but you appear to be a common drunk, with no resources, other than a pocket pistol you had no legal right to discharge. Someone haul him out of here."

Pim held a doubloon high over his head and walked to the

edge of the auction block. He held it where Philip could get a good look at the coin. The doubloon was a staggering sum of money, worth sixteen pieces of eight, or sixteen months' wages for a working man.

"Sold!" Philip said, grabbing the doubloon. "I'd stay and have a drink to celebrate your purchase, but I've pressing business back at my house." He walked behind Hester and pushed her fanny so hard she fairly flew off the platform and into Pim's arms.

Somewhere above the crowd a girl screamed, "No!"

13.

JACK AND ABBY Winter had ridden into town on his horse so she could watch her mother be sold. While Jack spoke to Pim, Abby made her way to the lodging house. Now they watched the humiliating spectacle while standing at an open window on the second floor there. When Pim bought Hester, Abby screamed again. Jack tried to calm her down before someone decided to summon the authorities.

"She's been bought by a homeless drunk!" Abby wailed. "Now what will become of my mum?"

"She'll be fine," Jack said.

"What? Fine? Can you possibly be this stupid? Just look at him down there, trying to talk to her. She must be terrified. See how she turns her face away from his rancid breath."

Jack was far more concerned about why Charlie Fine was in town. As Abby watched her mother, Jack's eyes tracked Charlie walking through the crowd, saw him grab the arm of Mayor Shrewsbury's aide, Barton Pike. When Jack saw Charlie pointing at Pim, he started running.

"Where are you going? Come back!" Abby yelled.

"Don't move! I'll be right back," Jack called over his shoulder.

He hit the stairs running, and made it to the courtyard in seconds. As he passed Pim, he pretended to wave at someone in the square, but said, "Pim, Hester, go to the lodging house.

Second floor. Run!"

Pim grabbed Hester by the arm and said, "Sorry, darlin', but trouble's afoot. Run!" They ran across the courtyard with Hester still in the halter with her hands tied. As the gawkers in the crowd watched them run, Jack doubled around the town square and came up behind Charlie and Barton Pike. He followed them as they went around the corner and approached the alley Jack knew would take them to the back entrance of Commander Dowling's quarters.

Jack followed the men into the alley and called their names. By the time they turned, he was upon them. He plunged a knife into Pike's rib and raked it sideways. Pike went down quietly, and when he hit the street, he was there to stay. One-Eyed Charlie Fine, by nature a nervous man, began shaking with fear. He fell to his knees and begged for mercy. Jack pulled him behind an empty water barrel.

"I'll have some information from you," Jack said, "and quickly."

"Anything!"

"What are you doing in town? Wait—don't lie to me."

Charlie had been about to do just that. Now it didn't seem sensible.

"The garrison up at Amelia has snuck down and surrounded the pirates."

"How could pirates get surrounded?"

"They're drunk and drugged."

"By the whores?"

Charlie nodded. "The pirates, once gathered, will be held."

"Where?"

"Top floor of my pub, the Blue Lagoon."

"Can't they jump out the window?"

"Window's too small. Even if they could get out, it's pretty

222

high. And anyway, they're guardin' the back."

"By how many men?"

"I don't know."

"To what purpose are they being held there?"

"They're going to be hung in my tavern one by one."

"On the first floor?"

Charlie nodded again.

"When?"

"It's already started. The rounding-up part anyway."

"What about the pirate ship?"

"They're sending *The Viceroy* to attack her."

"When?"

"At dawn."

As far as last words go, Charlie could have done worse. Jack made his way to the lodging house and found Abby and her mother whispering to each other. Both seemed dazed and distraught. Pim had gotten the halter off Hester and was working at the binding on her wrists.

Abby said, "Where did you go?"

Catching Pim's eye, Jack said, "I saw a man I know, and he meant to harm me and Mr. Pim, and some of our friends."

"Who's Mr. Pim?"

Pim smiled and gave a half-bow.

Abby backed up a step and shuddered. She looked at Jack.

"You actually know this…this person?"

"I do. And he's a close friend of mine."

"A friend? How can this be possible?"

Hester abruptly stopped crying and looked at Jack.

"Who are *you*?" she said. To Abby she said, "And how do you know him?"

"He's the father of my child," Abby said.

"He's *what*?" Hester's eyes dropped to Abby's chest a long

223

moment, then she slapped Jack full force across the cheek. Then she turned and slapped Abby nearly as hard.

When Pim said, "Jack's a good man," Hester slapped him as well.

Then Abby said, "Who the hell is Jack?"

Pim looked at Jack and shrugged his shoulders as if apologizing for blowing his cover.

"Look," Jack said. "There'll be plenty of time for explanations later on. Right now all you need to know is our lives are in danger, as are the lives of our friends. Hester, Mr. Pim is a bit raggedy now, but he cleans up right proper and he's wealthy and will make you a fine husband."

She looked at Pim and said, "I'm sorry I slapped you. It's been a vexing day."

"And getting worse by the moment," Jack said. He took Pim far enough aside that the women couldn't hear, and hurriedly repeated what Charlie had said. "I won't ask you to give up your land legs, but our mates are ambushed and need our help. Are you with me?"

"Aye, a course I am."

"Good. Now, listen. I've only got the one horse, so I've got to warn the ship. You'll have to walk to Sinner's Row and scout things out."

"What about the ladies? Leave 'em here?"

Jack looked at the women a moment, and sighed. "They'll slow us down, but you better take them."

"We could get 'em a room here."

Jack shook his head. "If her father comes, it won't go well for her and the baby."

"You truly be the one got her with child?"

"Let's just move along with our planning."

Pim smiled. "How much should I tell them?"

"Tell them everything."

"Hester might not want me if she knows my past."

Jack took a moment to survey his friend's appearance. "You think you could sink lower in her eyes?"

Pim shrugged.

Jack said, "Tell them what you like. But make sure they're safe."

"You got a plan?"

Jack nodded. "I'm working on it."

Pim nodded and said, "Okay, then. I guess we'll go together and listen for your whistle."

Jack walked over to Abby and cupped her chin in his hand. They kissed quickly, and when he broke away he looked her in the eyes. "I must warn my friends," he said.

"I'm coming with you."

"You can't. I'll have to ride hard. Also, I expect to pass your stepfather on the road, searching for you. So look sharp and stay with Mr. Pim."

Abby's face went white. "If Philip finds me he'll kill me."

"Mr. Pim won't allow it."

"You don't know Philip."

"And he don't know Pim. Okay, I'm off."

225

14.

JACK GALLOPED OUT of town and had gone about a mile when he ran into Philip Winter. Philip angled his horse across the path and held his musket across his chest, bidding Jack to stop.

"Who might you be?"

"Henry Ames. And you?"

"Philip Winter."

"You the man sold his wife an hour ago?"

"The same. Now I'm looking for my daughter."

"You planning to sell her too?"

Philip Winter sized Henry up. "Who knows you around here, Mr. Ames?"

"You do, for one."

Philip aimed his musket at Jack's face and pulled back the action.

"I'll have your horse, Henry, and you on the ground, face down until I decide what to do with you."

"I don't think so."

Jack jerked hard on his reign while kicking his horse's ribs. His horse slammed into Winter and Jack ducked below the gunshot. By then, Jack had his flintlock out and cocked in one hand, and Winter's reins in the other.

"I don't know why you'd wish to shoot a fellow traveler, or steal his horse, but it concerns me enough to ask you to dismount."

Winter reluctantly stepped down from his horse.

"What do you intend, sir?"

Jack wasn't sure. His first instinct was to kill Winter. But what would he do with the body? He didn't have time to deal with this right now.

"I'll take your horse with me," Jack said. "You'll find it at the river crossing, tied to a tree."

"I have urgent business. My daughter is missing."

"You'll have to delay the search. I'm sorry."

Winter nodded. "If I see you again, I'll kill you."

"In that case, I hope not to see you again. But since I'm bound for Georgia, I doubt our paths will cross."

"You're heading the wrong way for Georgia, sir."

"I'm making a detour. I'm a scout for *The Viceroy*, and have pirates to kill along the way."

"Wait! Why didn't you say this earlier? I'm part of the plot."

"What part is yours?"

"Why, creating the diversion so all the locals would be in town during the round-up."

Jack nodded. "But you intended all along to sell your wife, did you not?"

"Yes, of course. But the timing added some silver to my pocket."

"Mayor Shrewsbury?"

"The same. So, can I have my horse back?"

"One thing about being a scout. We don't trust anyone. You'll find your horse tethered to a tree by the clearing. You know the place?"

"Ought to, I live not a hundred yards from the spot."

"Very well. In the meantime, if I come across a young lady

227

I'll assume she's your daughter. What shall I tell her?"

"Tell her to get her ass home."

"Done, sir. Good luck to you."

"And you, sir."

15.

AS JACK APPROACHED George and Marie's home, he stopped his horse and whistled loudly. Within seconds he received a welcome whistle in return. The family gathered round. Johanna wore an angry expression on her face even as she cradled Rugby in her arms. The boys were chattering away about something, and George and Marie seemed puzzled. Jack looked at Rose.

"Can you really fly?"

All eyes had turned to Rose. She curled her lips into a humorless smile and said, "Is it the end of days, Henry?"

The way she said it sent a chill down Jack's spine.

Marie grabbed the boys by their shirts and dragged them to the house, kicking and screaming.

"Henry," said George. "She's our daughter. We've brought you in and trusted you. What are your intentions?"

Jack said, "You know nothing of the ambush at Sinner's Row?"

"What ambush?"

"You've heard no word of *The Viceroy* attacking *The Fortress*?"

"Of course not. Where have you gotten your information?"

"From the lips of a dying man."

Johanna, less angry now, said, "Henry, what is this about?"

"My men are being hung one by one at Sinner's Row. My

ship is about to be attacked."

"Your men? Your ship?" Johanna said.

George looked at the two girls.

"Henry's a privateer," he said.

Rose's face grew animated. "I *knew* it! And no ordinary pirate, are you, Henry? I'll tell you who he is, Johanna. He's Jack Hawley!"

George's face went white. "Could that possibly be true?"

Johanna had a different reaction. She seemed to be putting something together in her head. After a moment she said, "*Gentleman* Jack Hawley? Well that makes sense, now, doesn't it!"

Rose said, "Do you wish to ravish us, Jack Hawley?"

"Of course not!" Jack said. "Why would someone your age even think to say such a thing?"

"I'm an old soul, Henry. I'm sure George has told you that."

Indeed, George, who'd been known to exaggerate, had told Jack that Rose didn't appear to age like their other children. She looked the same four years ago when he found her as she did today.

"What are your intentions, Henry?" George said. "I mean, Mr. Hawley."

"George, we go way back. I like to think we're friends. I can see you might not have heard the news since the soldiers came from the north. But you're either with us or against us, and I'll respect which it is. But you need to cast your lot now, for time is running out on my men."

"I'm with you Henry," Johanna said.

"My family stands at your service," George said.

"And you, miss," Jack said to Rose. "Tell me truly. Can you fly?"

16.

JACK STARTED A smoke fire while George gathered all his weapons into saddlebags and tied them to four horses. Johanna put Rugby in a basket and tied it to her saddle.

Jack said, "Where's Rose?"

They looked around the yard. And when their eyes returned to the place they'd started, Rose was standing there, a scant four feet away.

"God's blood!" Jack swore.

Rose had rubbed gunpowder all over her face and rimmed her eyes with bright red paint. She stared straight ahead, as if in a trance.

"Jack?" George whispered tentatively.

"What?"

"We don't have any red paint here."

Jack turned to George. "Surely at some time you did."

"Never. No paint of any color. Where would I come by paint?"

"Where indeed?" Johanna said. She snapped her fingers and Rose came out of her trance-like state. From inside the basket, Rugby hissed savagely.

Jack said, "How did you know to do that?"

"Trial and error," Johanna said, and Jack felt another chill go down his spine.

He led his party of George, Johanna and Rose back up the

trail, past the crossing, beyond the town, and out to Sinner's Row.

About a hundred yards from the path that led to the small pier, Jack noticed two brightly colored soldier hats tied to trees six feet off the ground on either side of the road. He halted his horse, and the others fell in behind.

"What's that mean?" George said.

"It means they're dead," Rose said.

Jack nodded. "Mr. Pim must have found them guarding the trail. From the big pier, it looks like they're still here, standing guard."

"There'll be other guards, I'm sure," George said.

"If there are, we'll probably come upon their hats as well."

"How much danger are we in, Henry?" Johanna asked.

"It's okay to call me Jack, miss. That's my given name. I'm sorry for the lie."

"Jack," she said, softly. "I like that."

"How much involvement do you expect from Rose?" George said. "I can't let you put her in harm's way."

"I won't use her till it's safe."

"And when it's safe, what shall you have her do?"

Rose said, "Why, scare the life out of someone, right, Jack?"

Jack nodded absently, trying to decide if his plan had any chance of success. The entire rescue depended on a creepy little girl who might very possibly be crazy. Or delusional, if such was different. He didn't know if Rose was a witch or not, but he knew she had a terrifying laugh. If nothing else about her was supernatural, the laugh alone would likely suffice.

Jack looked around. It was getting on to dusk, but they were still two hours from dark. He chanced a light whistle and heard nothing in return. They climbed off their horses and led them into the woods until they got to a place where the foliage was thick enough to provide cover. They sat and waited.

An hour later, they heard a light return whistle. Jack and the others got to their feet, and Jack responded. Moments later, Abby raced into Jack's camp and threw her arms around him. Johanna arched an eyebrow, but waited politely to be introduced. When Abby started kissing Jack repeatedly, Johanna decided to take matters into her own hands. She started moving toward them, but stopped short as Hester entered the camp.

When Johanna saw Hester's face, she gasped, crossed herself, and spat. George did the same. Rugby arched her back, hissed, and jumped into Rose's arms.

Rose pointed at Hester and shouted, "Behold! The Devil's Mistress!"

Pim and Hester were even more startled by Rose.

"By the bones of Christ," Pim said. "Hell's cat has found its mother."

Abby was surprised that Henry wasn't kissing her back. She was even more surprised to find a thin young girl pulling her by the hair.

"Ow! Ow! Let go, you bitch!"

Johanna pulled her off of Jack before letting go of her hair. Abby tried to slap Johanna, but the younger girl evaded it. Abby looked at Jack.

"Who is this vile bitch?"

"This is Johanna," Jack said, warily.

"And who are you to pull my hair like a common street urchin?" Abby said to Johanna.

Johanna said, "I'm Jack's wife."

17.

TWO MONTHS EARLIER Jack had paddled up the Little River and ate dinner with the Stout family when a man called to them from outside the house. George opened the door and saw a man and woman, and behind them, a young girl tied to the horse rail.

"State your business," George said, as Jack passed him a musket. Jack pulled two flintlocks from his coat and held them crossed over his chest.

"My wife and I are trying to find the source of this feeling. If this is some herb you sell, we're here to trade for it."

George looked at Jack.

"Describe the feeling," George said, though he knew exactly what the man meant.

"I can't. It's just a feeling that's taken the pain from my gouty foot and my wife's back. It led me here. I'm Richard Bradford," the man said, "and this is my wife, Patience, and our daughter, Johanna."

"Why is she tied up?" George said.

"So she won't run off. She ain't right in the head, is what she is. We aim to get her married, though, if the price be right. Are you married, sir?"

George shook his head. After determining the Bradfords weren't likely to kill anyone, he introduced them to his family and Henry.

"Are you married, Henry?" Richard said.

"No. And don't intend to be."

Jack looked at Johanna across the yard. "She looks no more than nine."

"She is in fact twelve years old, as will be sworn by her mum and me. Why not come over and see for yourself what a delightful prize she'd be to a man who knows how to coax with a firm hand?"

"If you bring a lamp I'll lift her dress for you, sir," Patience said, "should you require a peek."

Jack had never hit a woman before, and never wanted to till now. But he kept his temper in check and said, "How much?"

"Twelve pounds sterling, sir, and worth every penny," Richard said.

"One for each year," Patience added.

Twelve pounds of silver was an exorbitant, ridiculous price for a dowry, which proved to Jack they thought him a fool. Jack said, "Go back inside. I'll speak to the child and give you my answer afterward."

Richard and Patience exchanged a glance, and Patience moved closer to Jack and whispered, "No offense, sir, but do you have the money with you? Because if so, we'd like to conclude the transaction before you put your hands on her. You might, no offense, lower her value by the degree of inspection you're planning to undertake."

While she spoke to Jack, Richard whispered something in the girl's ear. He left her with a stern glare, walked over to Jack and said, "I've told her not to scream should you decide to touch her. However, in the name of fairness, should you choose to sample her wares in a more deliberate manner, remuneration to the parents would be in order, due to her current state of innocence and the effect of wear and tear upon her future value."

Jack said, "I can assure you that I shall not be sampling this child's wares anytime soon, though I wish to speak to her a few moments.

"But you *are* interested?" Patience said.

"I am." Jack pressed a crown in each of their greedy hands and waited until they went inside. He picked up a lantern and crossed the yard to the horse post and untied the lead line around her neck and said, "If I untie your hands and promise not to touch you otherwise, will you walk with me a few steps and talk?"

Johanna nodded her head uncertainly.

Jack untied her and led her to the bench next to the watering tough. As they walked, he noticed her limping. They sat, and Jack asked some basic background questions and got yes or no answers in return. But when he asked, "How are you being treated by your father at home?" she said, "I cannot answer these questions without receiving severe punishment."

"I'll tell no one."

"There is something about you that makes me believe you," she said. "Something that calms me and makes me want to tell you what you seek to know. But he will certainly wish to know of what we spoke here, and he will beat the truth out of me."

Johanna turned her back to him and dropped the top of her shift so he could see her scars from being lashed.

"These marks are still wet with blood," Jack said.

"How else would they have got me to come?"

"I promise they will not beat you again."

"You'd have to marry me to keep that promise."

Jack sighed. "I would be inclined to do so if for no other

236

reason than to save you from your father's brutality. But I can't keep a wife. I travel and it's often dangerous places I go."

"You could marry me and keep me under any type of shelter that has a roof and walls and I'll improve the place and be there when you return from your travels. I'm not experienced in wifely ways, but I can chuck rocks well enough to kill small animals to skin and cook in a pot. I can clean and sew and will do as I'm told, though I will be grateful not to be beaten or cuffed about should I vex you unintentionally."

For one who seemed so shy at first she was proving to be a chatty little thing.

"You're tall enough," Jack said, "but you seem quite young. Are you even close to the age of consent?"

"I am twelve, sir, by almost nine months. There is proof from a midwife, as mine was a difficult birth."

"Are these two in fact your parents?"

"They are."

Now that Jack had her talking, the words spilled out of her. She told him that her father was a mean drunk who beat her older sister to death and made it appear to be an accident.

"He's nearly killed me twice," she added, "though not recently, as I have to gain strength again before trying to run away."

"And yet you keep trying."

"I do, sir."

"What's his drink of choice?" Jack asked, and Johanna gave him a funny look.

"Kill Devil," she said.

"Aye, that would do it," Jack said. Kill Devil was rum laced with gunpowder. It had been Blackbeard's favorite drink. "So your father drinks regular and beats you?"

"Regular enough."

237

"What about neighbors? Is there no one nearby to offer help?"

"We live deep in the woods where there's no one near to hear me scream. By day he keeps me tied to a lead line, which is convenient because he can use it to beat me with, should I move too slow in my chores. He threatens to hobble me if I run away again, and would have by now, except that he couldn't get a fair price for me. Of course, I am as horrid as I can be around them, thinking he might wish me gone enough to lower the price."

"I've met wood children before," Jack said. "How is it you learned such a fine manner of speech?"

"They weren't always like this. Before the poverty and drink seized him they were decent people. Mother was educated in London, taught my sister and me to read and write, taught my sister Lisbeth mostly, but Lisbeth taught me much. It was she who started the running away."

"What did he whisper to you just now?"

She looked around. Jack said, "It's all right. You can tell me."

"He told me if you turn me down, he's going to ruin me for all men."

Jack held up the lantern and saw the bruises running up and down her arms and legs. She had choke marks on her neck, and her cheekbones were in various stages of healing. A blood bruise covered half her right eye, and her lip was fat from a recent slap or punch. A line of dried blood started at the corner of her mouth and made a stain down her chin. She looked around again and whispered, "Though he quoted you twelve, he'd be happy with half that. Should you be interested in saving me, that is."

"You seem a lovely sort. A decent man wouldn't quibble

238

over the price."

"Are you a decent man, sir?"

"I like to think so."

"I'd like to have children someday."

Jack nodded. He took her to mean she feared being ruined by her father, should Jack turn her down.

"He'll eventually kill me," she said. Her body began shaking, and he realized she was crying. "Please, sir," she said. "I can butcher your kill and cut it down and salt it. I'm handy in the woods. I know some healing herbs and I'm good at finding tubers. If you save me I'll never give you reason to regret it."

Maybe it was the welts and bruises, or the unfairness of it all, or maybe just the rotgut from dinner buzzing in his brain. But Jack had asked to hear her tale of woe, and now he couldn't bear to hear another word. He took her by the hand and together they walked across the yard to George's front door, and when they opened it, Jack amazed himself by announcing he would marry Johanna Bradford that very night. He opened his kit and paid Richard and Patience Bradford twelve pounds sterling for their daughter's hand in marriage.

The only requirement for a legally valid marriage in 1710 was the completion of a marriage contract called a 'spousal,' and the exchange of vows. The entire process could be completed in minutes, with no witnesses required. For this reason, most young lovers were able to marry in secret. But Jack and Johanna had a number of witnesses. George prepared the contract, Jack and Johanna exchanged words, drinks were passed around, and then Johanna went with Marie to help put the child Steffan to bed.

Jack had half a mind to kill Johanna's parents where they

stood, but in deference to his bride he hustled them out of the house and told them to leave and never come back. With that chore out of the way, Jack sat down and worked out a payment for George and Marie to house Johanna and teach her to be a proper "helpmate," meaning a woman who knew how to keep a house and educate children.

"She can sleep in the guest room unless we have a visitor," George said.

Jack paid George two months in advance and said, "Her father claims she's wrong in the head, but I think he's the one that's crazy. But if she proves too much for you, I'll work out a different arrangement when I return."

The two men shook hands to seal the agreement, and Jack took some time to explain the arrangement to Johanna. Then he kissed her on the forehead, took a blanket and a bottle of rum out to the boat, climbed in and slept. The next morning he woke early, saddled one of George's horses, and went to the river crossing, hoping to see (but not intending to impregnate) his girlfriend, Abby Winter.

18.

NOW, IN THE woods, Pim waited patiently while Jack confirmed Johanna's claim. Abby called him a bastard, and Johanna lunged at her again.

Jack stepped between them and said, "Hush, you two. What's done is done and I'll do right by both of you."

"I don't see that possibility," Abby said, "since you're already married to this hellion, and I'm carrying your child."

"You've given her your seed?" Johanna said, incredulously. "How could you do this to me? I'm your wife. That seed is rightfully mine."

"I'd give it back if I could, you pasty-faced brat!" Abby said.

"Abby, that's enough! Johanna, it happened before I ever met you!"

"Oh," Johanna said.

"And again this very morning, if we're keeping a tally," Abby said.

Johanna glared at the older, prettier, pregnant girl a moment, then turned away and started running. Jack raced after her and found her lying on the ground, sobbing. Jack sat beside her and said, "This is not the best of circumstances, but we'll get through it. Right now we've some men to save, and I'll ask you to be civil for the time being. Too much noise at the wrong time could get us all killed."

Johanna looked him in the eyes. "You coupled with her this very morning? How could you, Jack?"

"I'm sorry I've hurt you. That's all I can say."

When they got back to the camp, Rose was grinning at him.

"Don't say a word," Jack warned.

Surprisingly, Hester had not spoken throughout the ordeal. She'd been treated far worse by men than what she'd seen between Jack and her daughter, and seemed content to stay out of it. When the camp had quieted down to an uneasy truce, Pim gave Jack his scouting report.

"There's eight soldiers guardin' the Blue Lagoon," he said, "and I don't know how many inside. Maybe ten, maybe twice that. Some're whorin', some're waitin' for the hangin'. Like you said, the men are all upstairs, so there must be guards on the steps as well. There were two guardin' the road on this side and two on the other, but they're arguin' for their souls with St. Peter at present. You formed a plan yet?"

"Has *The Fortress* moved?"

"Aye, she's backed out to deeper water, so she must've seen your signal. But she'll be a sittin' duck out there against *The Viceroy*, without men enough to work the guns."

"And the shore boats? Have the soldiers burned them?"

"Nay, they be right where they was."

"They must think they got all the pirates bottled up in one place."

"Aye, and most of 'em drunk or drugged halfway to Hades."

"In your experience, Pim, how superstitious are our mates?"

"This lot what's holed up in the Blue Lagoon? Worst I've seen."

"I agree. And what of soldiers in general, what do they fear most?"

Pim rubbed his beard. "I couldn't say for certain. But witches and faeries would scare any man, 'specially if they was comin' for their souls, I guess." He paused a minute and then said, "Why, you thinkin' of scarin' 'em somehow?"

Jack smiled.

"Then what're we waitin' for?" Pim said.

"Dark."

19.

THEY HAD EIGHT muskets between them, and a number of pistols and knives. Of the women, only Hester had fired a weapon before, and her experience was limited to pistols. They'd be going up against at least eight soldiers, two of whom stood behind the back of the building. There were at least twenty more inside, maybe more.

A sudden shriek pierced the night air, from inside the Blue Lagoon. Then several more followed. A gun fired, and things went quiet. Five minutes later, wild cheering erupted.

"What d'you think, Cap'n?" Pim said.

Jack set his jaw. "I think they've hung the first one."

Jack explained the plan twice, then arranged the participants and had them act it out. He offered several possible variations, and reviewed how they should react. By the time he felt comfortable with the details, it was dark. By then, if Jack was right about the screams and cheering, three more of his crew had been hung.

Since the Blue Lagoon was on a corner lot, there was nothing to prevent the soldiers from guarding the side, or going around the building to chat or drink with the guards in back. So Pim worked his way through the woods until he had a clear view of the far side. George and Rose worked their way to the edge of the woods on the near side, and got as close as they could to the Blue Lagoon while avoiding detection. At that point, Jack and Hester left the safety of the woods, followed by Abby and Johanna, trying to look like a regular colonial family that had wandered into the wrong area.

There were fifty yards of open space between the center of the woods and the back of the Blue Lagoon. The soldiers had set two sets of lamps on each corner behind the saloon, figuring to track any movement that blocked the light. But they'd grown lax in their duty, figuring all the pirates were caught and secured on the second floor, and the hanging had begun more than an hour ago and continued without interruption. So when Jack and his new "family" approached the soldiers and Hester cried out, "Sirs!" the guards were so startled they nearly shot each other.

Had Jack realized how carelessly they were guarding the back, he would have simply walked up and killed them. But that opportunity had passed, and now the soldiers were aiming muskets at them. The two girls peeked out from behind.

"Who are you?" one said, "And what are you doing out here without a lamp?"

The soldier's breath was heavy with liquor.

"We came down the beach some time ago, headed for St. Alban's," Jack said. "My wife had a pain in her chest and we went to the woods to seek an herb. Then we got lost and stayed that way until we seen your lights. Can you say if there be a doctor nearby?"

The other soldier walked to the corner, picked up one of the lamps, and brought it back. He held it up to Hester's face and cursed, almost dropping it.

"What the hell is wrong with your woman?"

"As I say, she's sufferin'."

"You said her chest was paining her. Maybe we should

take a look."

Jack said, "Go ahead and show them, dear. Maybe they can help."

"Aye, we've seen lots of titties. We know how they'd look should somethin' be wrong with 'em."

As Hester began working the buttons the soldiers drew in for a closer look. But as she opened the top of her dress, Rugby shrieked and jumped out with claws flying. Neither soldier had time to react, as Jack's knife made short work of them. A moment later, George and Rose ran up to him, panting. Jack and George stripped and changed into the guards' uniforms, then helped Hester, Johanna and Abby drag the bodies back to the woods. Rugby followed them with something hanging from his mouth. Turned out she'd ripped one of the guard's ears off and was saving it to eat later.

Rose hid herself under Jack's coat and scrunched up against the back of the building where the light was dim.

With their jobs done, Hester, Johanna and Abby sought shelter in the woods. Pim's whistle told Jack that he had them covered, should anyone approach from the far side of the building.

Based on what Pim had said, Jack had reason to believe his men could sense that he was nearby. This would give them courage, should they regain their faculties. What Jack didn't understand was Pim's comment that, with Jack beneath the window, the men would quickly start sobering up and lose their grogginess from the drugs.

Just then, another burst of cheering emanated from the building, which meant they were down five men. Moments later, two drunken soldiers made their way around the far corner and picked up the remaining lamp. They were in their long johns and one was wearing his soldier's cap backwards.

Jack hollered, "Here, let me give you a hand." He moved quickly to them, and listened as they told him about the quality of the hookers and beer inside. He interrupted their stories with his knife. George ran over and helped drag the new bodies out of view.

Four down, and two of them guards. Leaving six guards out front, and maybe two dozen soldiers inside. Plus however many were entertaining whores in the building next door.

By Jack's calculation there were probably more pirates in the Blue Lagoon than soldiers. Good. As he was about to begin the tricky part of his plan, he heard Pim's danger whistle.

"Rose," he whispered. "Stay down."

A soldier had made his way down the side of the building to check on the other guards. As he turned the corner, George, on his knees, swung the butt of his musket as hard as he could into the soldier's kneecaps. The soldier let out a scream that died in his throat when George cut his neck. Two of the other guards at the front corner heard their comrade's scream and ran to the back of the building to investigate. George was hovering over the body, pretending to give it aid. As the soldiers approached, George turned toward them, revealing two drawn pistols, which he used to shoot them. Then he tossed the pistols to Jack for reloading, and shouted for help.

The three remaining guards raced around the building. As they approached, George shouted, "One pirate, running. He's killed these two, but he's out of ammunition!" George pointed to the sand dunes. Two of them made for the sand dune, the third started running to warn the soldiers inside.

It wasn't necessary, since they'd all heard the gunfire. A half-dozen soldiers joined the guard out front, heard the report of an unarmed lone pirate running through the sand dunes, and rejoined the soldiers inside who were conducting the hangings. By then, Pim had shot the two on the sand dune, and George and Jack lured the remaining guard out of view and stabbed him quietly, then propped the body against the wall to make it appear he was passed out.

George stood guard out front while Jack entered the whorehouse. Moments later Jack returned and reported there were no soldiers inside. He waited for Pim's whistle. When it came, Jack went to the back of the building and told Rose it was time. She climbed out from under Jack's coat and stood below the second-floor window, whose base was about sixteen feet off the ground. She lifted her arms over her head. At that moment, Jack would have given anything to see what she was going to do and how she planned to do it. But George needed help, so he reluctantly turned the corner and ran to the front of the building to provide it.

Then the sound started.

20.

BECAUSE IT WAS dark, and the remaining two lamps inadequate to offer Pim or the women a clear view of what transpired next, and because for the rest of their lives no one believed the pirates' version, since admittedly they were drunk or drugged at the time, and because there was only one sober person who knows exactly what happened, and since she was the one who did it, history never recorded what happened that night behind the Blue Lagoon.

But according to the captured pirates, she flew.

Rose flew.

Or at least, she lifted herself off the ground.

As she raised herself higher and higher into the warm night air behind the Blue Lagoon, she began speaking words that Jack had never heard in any of his travels. Indeed, she seemed to be speaking two or three different languages at the same time, and her voice was huge and shrill and powerful, and louder than any storm. As the sounds from her voice grew louder and louder still, the pirates covered their ears and fell to their knees and prayed for mercy. By then the sound had become a high-pitched wail, a shrieking, ear-splitting cyclone of a sound that shattered the second-floor window.

Jack's superstitious men took one look at the demon-possessed child hovering twenty feet off the ground and became horror-struck. It seemed to be the coming of the dead.

They cried and moaned and gnashed their teeth and crossed themselves and pushed their fingers deep into their ears. Such was the chaos that every soldier on the first floor scrambled up the stairs to see what was happening. At that precise moment, while the hallway and stairs were filled with soldiers, Jack charged through the front door with George and the two began shooting. Then, according to the drunken survivors, Rose opened her eyes and they glowed reptilian yellow, with a vertical black line in the center. She switched to English and spewed forth such vile oaths and imprecations that Jack's thirty-five hardened pirates crashed through the door and charged into the soldiers with wild abandon, like deer running from a raging fire.

Finding themselves caught off guard, trampled by the fleeing pirates, the soldiers were unable to fire their weapons for lack of space to point them. With upwards of forty men on the staircase, screaming and pushing to escape, it finally crashed to the floor. By then, Pim had joined his friends and together they emptied their weapons into the enemy. When the pirates realized Jack and Pim were killing soldiers, they warmed to the task and killed their share.

A half-hour later, the pirates were settled in the landing boats, waiting for their captain. To a man, they refused to look in Rose's direction, though Jack himself had vouched for her. Had they looked at Rose, they'd have seen Rugby perched on her shoulder, looking very calm.

Jack shook Pim's hand, clapped him on the shoulder and said, "Good luck to you, and your wife-to-be. I'll miss you."

Pim said, "And you as well. Godspeed!"

Jack hugged Johanna, thanked George, kept his distance from Rose, and waved to Hester. Then he and Abby Winter climbed into one of the boats and they all headed out to sea.

After twenty minutes of rowing, Jack instructed them to sing pirate songs so the skeleton crew would know to come fetch them.

Within moments of boarding, Abby started in.

"What manner of conditions are these?" she said. "You men live like pigs! I've never smelled anything like it! Have you no pride?"

She approached Cook, who was busy working at his enormous pot. Scattered around him on the deck floor were dead pigeons, turtles, fish, palm hearts, pickled eggs, onions, cabbage, wine, and some ingredients she had never seen before, nor cared to see again.

"What is that dreadful stench?" she said.

"Salamagundi, miss," said Cook.

"What's that?"

"Dinner."

"Why, it smells like the bowels of a goat. Like the very breath of death!"

"Well, the smell's the best part."

"God help us all."

Cook looked at Jack. "Shall I toss her overboard for you?" he said.

"She's new. I'll get her below decks, get her settled in," Jack said.

Abby attempted to follow Jack down the steps into the hold, but began retching. She grabbed her mouth and reversed course and puked on the deck, five feet from Cook's pot.

"Is that your contribution to the pot, miss?" Cook said.

"Oh, you wretched, wretched beasts!" she cried.

Halfway down the steps, Jack sighed. This was why they normally didn't allow women on board ship. He climbed back up the stairs and joined her. "You feel better now?"

"What's going on here?" Abby said. "You can't tell me you live like this!"

"I can and we do."

"But you can't! I mean, you don't actually *sleep* at the bottom of those steps!"

"Aye, miss, we do. As you will, and gladly, when a big enough storm's afoot."

"What has happened down there to make such a vile odor?"

"Happened?"

"I mean, it's an unnatural smell."

"That's what you said about the soup."

"Nay, I was wrong. Whatever happened below decks is far worse than the soup. I'd rather be reamed by Philip Winter's pink pizzle than step foot down there again."

"Truly?"

"I mean, explain it to me, Jack. Surely there's a better solution to be had."

"Well, it's hot and humid, and the ship is old, and made of wood. That smell you're referring to is a mixture."

"A mixture of what?"

"It's no secret to any seafaring man. It's bilge water that's gone bad over the course of time, mixed with the smell of unbathed bodies, rotten fish and meat, and livestock excrement."

"What do you mean, livestock?"

"Well, of course we keep pigs and chickens and goats and other animals alive down there."

"Alive?"

"Sometimes we're at sea for months. You can salt your meat, but it goes rotten after a few weeks, so we keep the livestock to be butchered when needed."

"And you and your men sleep among the pigs, do you?"

"Oh, no, miss. They're on the orlop, the lowest level. We sleep just above them. But their waste goes through the boards and down into the bottom to mix with the bilge water, so it don't often smell so sweet. As to the livestock, believe me, after a couple weeks at sea, when the biscuits are hard and full of black-headed weevil maggots, you'll be thankful for fresh meat."

"Where do you keep your water?"

"In them barrels over there."

Abby crossed the deck and lifted one of the lids and smelled.

"Ugh! Rancid! Disgusting!" she said.

"Well, it's fresh now," Jack said. "But it don't take long for it to go stale on you." Growing philosophical, he added, "and that's a taste we never get used to."

"You don't?"

"No."

"And why's that?"

"Because it keeps gettin' worse."

Abby shook her head at the magnitude of it. "There's bound to be rats running throughout the bottom deck."

"Aye, miss, and everywhere else as well. And roaches and water snakes and thousand leggers and all sorts of nighttime crawly things."

"Can't you fumigate the ship?"

"Well, we do."

"You do."

"Yes, miss."

"And how is that accomplished? I'm asking because whatever you're doing, it's not working."

"Well, we pour burning pitch down there from time to

time and make them that's being punished mop it around. But that ain't a permanent solution, and the chickens don't like it."

"They don't? How do you know, do you speak chicken?"

"No, miss, but their eggs come out black for a long time after. I think they peck at the pitch, but I can't say for sure."

Abby frowned. What's going to happen now?"

"We'll have some dinner and prepare for tomorrow's battle."

"Battle? With *The Viceroy*? Can't we just leave harbor now and outrun them?"

"A course we could, but where's the fun in that?"

"Fun?"

21.

FRIGHTENED LIZARDS SKITTERED across the deck as Captain Jack pushed open the cabin door and summoned his men to the main deck to review his battle strategy. It was an hour before dawn, and his crewmen, fortified by the rum they'd consumed the previous night, were itching for battle. The blanket of heavy fog that had hung about ten feet above the water most of the night was starting to dissipate, and those who looked directly above the ship were able to see stars littering the blue-black sky.

Captain Jack had his men fill two shore boats with pitch, and lower them into the water on the leeward side of the ship. He summoned his four best swimmers and instructed them to jump in the water and hold onto the sterns, two to a boat. Then he lowered two lit lanterns to the men, and had them carefully place the lanterns in the front and center of each boat.

The men kicked their legs and pushed the boats a hundred yards northeast and southeast of *The Fortress*. When they'd got into position, they held onto the sterns to wait for *The Viceroy*. These were brave men, since the waters off St. Alban's were popular breeding grounds for sand sharks. Jack knew *The Viceroy* would attack at dawn, and almost certainly from the east, for two reasons: first, because that would put a giant ball of sun in the pirates' eyes, and second, they'd be coming fast, with the wind at their backs, presenting a vertical target for Jack's guns, which would make it almost impossible to score a direct hit. The good news was *The Viceroy* couldn't attack from that attitude. She'd have to turn broadside to point her guns at *The Fortress*, and therein lay Jack's window of advantage.

Jack walked to the prow to check on Abby. She'd made good on her refusal to step foot below decks, so Jack had gotten some men to overturn a shore boat for her to climb under, which gave her a less offensive shelter to sleep in. He would have loved to couple and cuddle with her in their last night, but doing so would have been a violation of his own rule against sexual relations aboard ship.

"Did you sleep well, miss?"

"No."

"Well, it should have been comfortable, with them sails folded up for you like a feather bed."

"I kept hearing frightening noises all night and feared I'd be bit by something horrid and die."

She started to cry.

"And now there's to be a battle and you're likely to be killed and if me and our baby happen to survive, what would become of us? If your men win the battle, I'll probably be ravished to death. If they lose, I'll likely be hung, or returned to my stepfather."

"Aye, even the most comfortable bed means little with thoughts such as these to nag you. But I have a solution for your fears."

"What's that?"

"If I live, none of your worries will happen."

"Then do so!"

Jack gave her hand a squeeze and went below decks to

check on the guns. Ship cannons ranged from 500 to over 1,500 pounds, and required between four and eight men to handle them. Jack preferred 800 pound cannons, since they could be managed by four well-trained men. He didn't have enough men to man all his cannons, but he would only be using one side of the ship today, since he was so close to shore.

"One rope should hold them," Jack said.

His cannon crew agreed that the waters were calm enough to use one rope per gun. On stormy seas they used two, though it slowed down the process of pulling the cannons away from the gun ports, reloading them, and pushing them back in place to fire. But two ropes prevented one of the biggest dangers a cannon crew faced in battle: severing the rope that held the cannons in place. When that happened in a pitching sea, an 800 pound cannon rolling around at high speed could mow down an entire crew.

Jack watched as the sea monkeys did their jobs, sea monkeys being the young boys who were assigned the worst jobs on ship, such as pumping out the bilge with a bellows. On battle days, they'd have to scamper down to the lower decks and retrieve cannon balls, which on Jack's boat were light at eighteen pounds. Of course today they were using chain shot, which consisted of two cannon balls connected by a chain. When fired, these worked like a mace, cutting down masts to render the enemy ship helpless. But two balls and a chain in each cannon more than doubled the crew's workload.

Jack wished his men good luck and thanked them for their duty. Then he went back up top and got his four musicians together and ordered them to scatter sand over the deck to soak up the blood that was expected to flow. Nothing worse than fighting a battle on a slick deck with the boat pitching at funny angles due to wind, steering, and incoming cannon fire.

Once that had been accomplished, he had them stack ammunition in various areas of the deck. Finally, they soaked dozens of blankets in water in preparation for putting out fires.

"Look sharp!" Jack called to the helmsman, for once the battle started, the enemy would try to shoot the helmsman first, in order to nullify the steering.

"Sail ho!" cried Roberts from the crow's nest.

Just as Jack predicted, *The Viceroy* was moving fast under full sail, heading directly toward them from the east. Roberts gave the signal to the swimmers, and they knocked their lamps over and lit the pitch. The sailors on *The Viceroy* would see the smoke, but it wouldn't dissuade them from attacking, since they were under the impression they were attacking a boat manned by a skeleton crew.

As she approached, Jack had his men stand quiet. Roberts gave the signal and the swimmers began kicking their legs, propelling the flaming boats toward each other. By the time *The Viceroy*'s captain realized the burning boats were part of a plan, it was too late. He ordered the boat to come about sooner than the crew expected, and they got caught with their sails fluttering. That gave Jack's men not only a broad target to shoot at, but also a slow-moving one. Four cannons fired on Jack's command, and the other four crews watched to see the result. One chain shot hit the bottom of the ship, the other three fell short. As the four crews began reloading, the other four adjusted the height and fired.

Three direct hits, but no mast damage. *The Viceroy* had made the adjustment, and stood parallel to *The Fortress*, separated by some fifty yards of ocean. As she made ready to fire her cannons she was struck once, then a second time by Jack's burning shore boats. The swimmers had built up enough speed that upon impact, the shore boats knocked yards of flaming pitch onto the fore and aft hulls: a death blow to a wooden ship like *The Viceroy*.

By then two of Jack's cannon crew had reloaded. They fired. One of them found their target, the main mast. When the mast was cut, everyone on *The Viceroy* felt the impact, and it delayed their cannon crews a few seconds.

Which was all Jack needed.

Two more crews were reloaded, and Jack ordered them to fire, which they did, aiming at *The Viceroy*'s gun ports. The impact was sufficient to delay their shot again, and now, with no main mast, burning from both ends, she was a sitting duck. Jack's first four crews began reloading while the second four cannon crews fired and destroyed four more gun ports.

Jack ordered two shore boats lowered to pick up his swimmers. While that was going on, *The Viceroy* finally managed to get off three cannon shots, but two missed and the third caused only minor damage. Jack had his crew come about and they circled the wounded ship until they were at a right angle to it. From there, Jack's guns could shoot but *The Viceroy*'s could not. Jack waited until all eight guns were ready, then he gave the signal, and all eight sent chain shot directly into the bow. *The Viceroy* lurched downward. In one last act of determination, her crew attempted to hurl grenades, but *The Fortress* was out of range. Realizing the battle was lost, *The Viceroy*'s captain ran up the white flag, but by then she was in flames to the point that Jack's men could do nothing but watch her burn. Enemy sailors screamed and jumped into the water, hoping to swim their way to shore, but Jack doubted any would make it.

Martin, who in Pim's absence had been promoted to quartermaster, said, "Want me to lower some boats? We can follow and shoot them as they swim."

Jack said, "No, let them be."

"But what if they make it to shore?"

"In my mind, any sailor who can swim that far in these conditions deserves to live."

22.

JACK TRAINED HIS spyglass on the town of St. Alban's. Having heard the cannon fire a scant half-mile from shore, hundreds of residents had gathered to witness the naval battle. Now they began dispersing, fearing the worst. Jack ordered his men to bring the ship into port at downtown St. Alban's. Once there, a boat was lowered, and ten men rowed to the main pier under a flag of truce. Forty men, Mayor Shrewsbury, and half as many women and children came out to the pier to see what might happen next.

The men in the boat tied her off and stepped onto the pier. Nine held pistols in each hand. The tenth came to the front and began to speak.

"My surname is Martin, and I'm quartermaster of *The Fortress*. We're here under flag of truce to explain why we feel wronged by your city, and how we intend to respond. Our men were enjoying shore leave at Sinner's Row as we've done many times these past four years. This time, with the direct knowledge and cooperation of your mayor (Martin pointed to Mayor Shrewsbury), a number of our crew were drugged, and without warning or explanation, captured and held against their will at the Blue Lagoon, where soldiers from the garrison at Amelia Island began summarily executing them.

We defeated the soldiers, only to be attacked moments ago by *The Viceroy*, sailing under the colors of Florida Colony, with the full knowledge and cooperation of Mayor Shrewsbury. For these reasons, Jack Hawley, captain of *The Fortress*, has ordered the town of St. Alban's decimated."

The townspeople gasped and began murmuring to each other.

"I've come to tell you that if you have any weapons, you're to lower them to the ground."

"What do you mean, 'decimated?'" the mayor said, in as haughty a voice as he could muster.

Martin pointed to *The Fortress*. "As you can see, our ship has anchored broadside, exposing her guns."

He pulled the white flag out of its holder in the stern, waved it high over his head, then replaced it.

"I just signaled Captain Hawley, which means you have exactly one hour to evacuate the downtown area before it begins raining cannonballs. Captain Jack is already lowering shore boats filled with angry pirates bent on revenge. They'll wait a hundred yards from shore until the firing stops. At that point, should you stay, God help you all."

Mayor Shrewsbury cleared his throat and said, "Now listen here, you can't just destroy the whole town. These are innocent citizens and I'm an appointed official, acting under direct orders from the governor. It would be treason not to do as I'm told, just as you would not go against orders from your captain, Jack Hawley."

Martin said, "You've got about fifty-eight minutes. If I were you, I'd start moving things along."

The mayor said, "Surely there is a way to come to an understanding with Captain Hawley. I'm sure we could gather up a substantial amount of money, food and medicine. We could pay you in return for sparing our town."

Martin said, "You're suggesting the town pay a ransom?"

"A ransom, yes. That's exactly what I'm suggesting." Mayor Shrewsbury said, worriedly. "We've lost your trust, but we're willing to sacrifice, if need be, to regain it. How say you to that?"

"It's not for me to say, but I expect Captain Hawley would decline, since he intends to destroy the town and take the spoils anyway."

Mayor Shrewsbury said, "If there's no understanding to be had, perhaps we should take matters into our own hands. We have enough manpower here on the pier to kill the whole boatload of you."

With that, he raised his hand and forty men aimed their weapons at the ten pirates. To be precise, thirty-eight men aimed their weapons at the pirates. The other two were George Stout and Mr. Pim, and they were armed to the teeth. As the women and children moved off the pier at a high rate of speed, George and Pim began working their way behind the mob.

Martin said, "We've come under the flag of truce. Are we not gentlemen?"

"Not when you intend to destroy our town, sir. And if we're to die anyway, I'd like to hear one reason why we shouldn't kill ten pirates now, while the killing's good."

The men from the town cocked their muskets. Pim and George had a pistol in each hand and several more loaded and tucked into their coats. They wouldn't be able to kill them all, but they'd probably get eight or nine before having to use their knives.

"I'll give you a good reason," Martin said. "If you put up any resistance, Jack Hawley will not only destroy the town, he and his men will hunt you down, nail you to trees, and make you watch as they rape your wives, daughters and livestock. Then they'll kidnap your sons and turn them into sea monkeys."

One citizen said, "Rape our livestock?"

"The nicer livestock, yes."

One by one, the men lowered their weapons to the ground and stepped aside as the pirates kicked them into the water.

"Wise decision," Martin said. "And you now have approximately fifty-three minutes to evacuate the town."

The men began running off the pier, but stopped when they saw a young girl walking toward them carrying a kit in one hand and a white flag in the other.

Martin shouted, "What have we here?"

The men parted as the girl walked toward the pirates. They filed in behind her to hear what she had to say.

"Who are you, miss?" Martin said.

"Abby Winter, sir."

"State your business."

"I've come to offer myself to Captain Jack Hawley, if he'll spare the town in return."

Martin laughed. "One girl worth the whole town? Surely you jest."

"Not just a girl," she said, "but a girl of pure heart and noble spirit."

"If Captain Jack wants such a girl he will surely take her against her will. What say ye to that?"

"Is your captain not called *Gentleman* Jack Hawley? It is said he respects valor and—"

Martin held up his hand. "Speak not a moment."

The pirates huddled up and talked among themselves a few minutes. Then Martin again pulled the white flag from the boat and waved it high over his head, replaced it, and approached the girl. "Get in the boat, miss, and I'll let you plead your case to Jack Hawley." To the others he said, "If the ship hoists anchor and sets sail, Hawley accepts. If the ship fires her guns, he don't."

Martin and the girl climbed into the front of the boat and sat, and the pirates took their places and began rowing. After they'd gone about ten yards from the dock, Martin turned and shouted, "Hear me now! This Abby Winter is a brave girl! Pure of heart and of noble spirit, yet not one of ye thought to ask what might happen to her aboard our ship! You are cowards all! Shame on you! Shame, and a curse on your wretched town!"

The pirates stopped rowing. The boat rocked with each quiet swell of waves. Several moments passed. The men on the pier hung their heads.

Demonstrating remarkable balance, Martin stood to his full height in the boat and repeated, "Shame on you! A one-hundred...nay, a *three*-hundred-year curse on your town begins today!"

PREVIEW
5
DONOVAN
CREED
Be careful what you wish
for... you might just get it!
WISH LIST
2 MILLION COPIES AND COUNTING...
JOHN LOCKE

PROLOGUE

Donovan Creed

WE'D MET ON the Internet, exchanged emails, and she was married. But she accepted a dinner date anyway, and showed up. We toasted, talked, flirted unmercifully, shared a sissy dessert, and then went to my room for a nightcap. The drinks came and went, then we cuddled and kissed and I started to undo her blouse and she said, "I can't."

"Can't what?"

"Do this."

"Why not?"

She looked as though she didn't mean it, but said, "It's not right."

"Oh."

"Don't be mad."

"I'm not. I thought things were going well. I was wrong."

"It's not that. Really, it's just, we shouldn't do this."

"It's me?"

"No, of course not! You're incredible! I've had a wonderful time."

"But things could have gone better tonight. For you, I mean."

"No, that's not it. Look, I promise, it's not you."

I nodded. "Can I ask you something?"

"Yes, of course."

"Did you buy a new bra and panties before coming here?"

"What?"

"I'm just curious. You don't have to show me or anything, I was just wondering if your underwear is new."

She blushed. "It is. It's new."

"And you bought it when?"

"What difference does it make?"

I said nothing.

She said, "Two days ago. What's your point?"

"So…two days ago you thought it might be okay for you to take your clothes off if things went well between us, but now it's not okay. And the only thing that's different is we've met and spent some time together, which you say was incredible."

She started to say something but changed her mind, then closed her eyes tightly and winced, as if trying to com-pute something mathematically.

"Oh, hell," she said, "Let's just do it and get it over with!"

"Let's," I said.

I started working the buttons on her blouse with renewed vigor, giving her little time to regret her decision. I got the damn thing off, along with her bra, meaning, I'd just gotten to the good part when my cell phone vibrated on the nightstand.

"You need to get that?" she said.

I grabbed my knife from under the pillow and plunged it through the center of the phone in a motion so quick it should have impressed the shit out of her. In retrospect I guess she hadn't expected the knife or my ability to use it.

She ran to the door screaming, clutching her bra and blouse to her chest. She was fidgety, and it took a while to get the

2

door unlocked, but when she realized I wasn't chasing her she paused to put her clothes on, while keeping a wary eye on me.

I was aware of all this, but I was more interested in my cell phone.

It was still ringing.

I pried the knife loose and answered it.

"Creed."

"Mr. Creed, this is Buddy Pancake. I'm in trouble."

To the girl in my room I said, "Wait. You lost an earring." It was a large gold hoop, probably bought at the same time she bought the underwear. I slid it on the blade of my knife and hurled it in her direction. She shrieked as it stuck in the door frame and vibrated back and forth. It was a good throw, one that should have dazzled her, landing as it had a mere two inches from her face.

"Buddy," I said, "You're a pain in the ass."

"Sorry, Mr. Creed."

My date angrily tried to pry the knife out of the door frame, but I'd thrown it too hard. She gave up, opened the door, and, rather rudely I thought, flipped her middle finger at me before leaving.

I said, "What kind of trouble have you gotten yourself into this time, Buddy?"

"The worst kind."

I sighed. "Where are you?"

INTRODUCTION

ON APRIL 8, 2010, custom motorcycle builder Jesse James was voted "The Most Hated Man in America," for cheating on America's Sweetheart, actress Sandra Bullock.

The story broke three days after Sandra won the Oscar for Best Actress for her performance in *The Blind Side*.

The Academy Awards had been held Sunday, March 7, at Hollywood's Kodak Theatre. In attendance that night were a number of famous beauties, including Mariska Hargitay, Kate Winslet, Maria Menounos, Demi Moore, Jinny Kidwell, Amanda Seyfried, and Charlize Theron.

If you're lucky enough to be a world famous actress, *and* one of the world's most beautiful women, you might not say it out loud, but secretly you know you can have any man on the planet.

For this reason, the entire world would be stunned to know that five days after Sandra Bullock won her Oscar, a balding, pudgy, middle class nobody named Buddy Pancake managed to do something only three men in the entire world had done.

He fucked Jinny Kidwell.

How did a man like this wind up in bed with Jinny Kidwell? Simple.

He wished it.

1.

THIS WHOLE THING started the way things often do: a few guys hanging out together on a Sunday afternoon, talking about pussy.

It's early March, and we're three underachievers, soft, wimpy, mid-management worker bees, sitting in the basement of my split-level ranch, in the room I like to call my office. There's an old college couch in here, and a black, faux-leather bean bag chair. An ancient, but working, TV sits atop a maple desk I salvaged from my neighbor's yard sale last summer. It's not fancy, but it's mine, and has a matching chair. The room's only window shows half dirt, half sky. It's split horizontally, and the top half pushes open about six inches, just enough to let the weed smoke out.

By way of introduction, I'm Buddy Pancake.

I'll pause a minute, while you bust my balls. Go ahead, ask me if Pancake is my real name.

It is.

Ask me "What's Mrs. Butterworth?"

I don't know. What, maybe five bucks?

Hilarious.

Move along to where I live.

Yeah, that's right. The Pancake House.

I know. You got a million more.

Do me a favor. Put the pancake thing on hold while I tell my story. You won't be sorry, it's a helluva story.

For five days I was the luckiest man in the world.

And then I wasn't.

DONOVAN CREED

DONOVAN CREED works as an assassin for an elite branch of Homeland Security. When he isn't killing terrorists, he moonlights as a hit man for the mob, and tests torture weapons for the Army. Donovan Creed is a very tough guy.

To discover more – and some tempting special offers – why not visit our website:
www.headofzeus.com